BARRY HUTCHISON

INVISIBLE FIENDS

THE DARKEST CORNERS

HarperCollins *Children's Books*

First published in Great Britain by
HarperCollins *Children's Books* 2012

HarperCollins *Children's Books* is a division of HarperCollins*Publishers* Ltd,
77-85 Fulham Palace Road, Hammersmith, London W6 8JB

The HarperCollins *Children's Books* website address is
www.harpercollins.co.uk

1

ISBN 978-0-00-731520-8

Typeset in Futura by Palimpsest Book Production Limited,
Falkirk, Stirlingshire

MIX
Paper from
responsible sources
FSC™ C007454

For my son, Kyle, the inspiration for this series.

This is it. Kyle versus Dad. You against me.

May the best man win...

PROLOGUE

What had I expected to see? I wasn't sure. An empty street. One or two late-night wanderers, maybe. But not this. Never this.

There were hundreds of them. *Thousands*. They scuttled and scurried through the darkness, swarming over the village like an infection; relentless and unstoppable.

I leaned closer to the window and looked down at the front of the hospital. One of the larger creatures was tearing through the fence, its claws slicing through the wrought-iron bars as if they were cardboard. My breath fogged the glass and the monster vanished behind a cloud of condensation. By the time the pane cleared the *thing* would be inside the hospital. It would be up the stairs in moments. Everyone in here was as good as dead.

The distant thunder of gunfire ricocheted from somewhere near the village centre. A scream followed – short and sharp, then suddenly silenced. There were no more gunshots after that, just the triumphant roar of something sickening and grotesque.

I heard Ameena take a step closer behind me. I didn't need to look at her reflection in the window to know how terrified she was. The crack in her voice said it all.

'It's the same everywhere,' she whispered.

I nodded, slowly. 'The town as well?'

She hesitated long enough for me to realise what she meant. I turned away from the devastation outside. 'Wait... You really mean *everywhere*, don't you?'

Her only reply was a single nod of her head.

'*Liar!*' I snapped. It couldn't be true. This couldn't be happening.

She stooped and picked up the TV remote from the

day-room coffee table. It shook in her hand as she held it out to me.

'See for yourself.'

Hesitantly, I took the remote. 'What channel?'

She glanced at the ceiling, steadying her voice. 'Any of them.'

The old television set gave a faint *clunk* as I switched it on. In a few seconds, an all-too-familiar scene appeared.

Hundreds of the creatures. Cars and buildings ablaze. People screaming. People running. People *dying*.

Hell on Earth.

'That's New York,' she said.

Click. Another channel, but the footage was almost identical.

'London.'

Click.

'I'm... I'm not sure. Somewhere in Japan. Tokyo, maybe?'

It could have been Tokyo, but then again it could have been anywhere. I clicked through half a dozen more channels, but the images were always the same.

'It happened,' I gasped. 'It actually happened.'

I turned back to the window and gazed out. The clouds above the next town were tinged with orange and red. It was already burning. They were destroying everything, just like *he'd* told me they would.

This was it.

The world was ending.

Armageddon.

And it was all my fault.

TWELVE HOURS EARLIER...

Chapter One

THE BEGINNING OF THE END

The world changed.

It happened in an instant, but it felt like an age as my mind swirled with everything I had just gone through. Running from the screechers. My battle with the Beast. Discovering that Ameena wasn't real – had *never* been real. But through it all one thought loomed larger than all the others.

My dad. A tape recorder. A *bang* from the tinny speaker as he shot and murdered my mum. His face, smiling at me. Leering, laughing.

And then an explosion inside of me. A rage, like nothing I had ever felt before. He had killed my mum. He had made me listen to her dying screams. And then he had run away.

But no matter how fast he ran, it would never be fast enough. I was coming for him. This, finally, would be the end.

Shadows engulfed me as I arrived in the Darkest Corners, the Hell-like alternate reality where all forgotten imaginary friends go. The world I'd left behind had been blanketed by snow, but here the ground was awash with filth and stagnant puddles.

The buildings around me were the same, but different. These were crumbling relics of those back in the real world, all boarded-up windows or burned-out shells. They were barely visible in the faint glow of the moon.

I spun on the spot, searching for any sign of my dad. He'd had only a few seconds' head start, so he should have been somewhere close by. I peered into the gloom, trying to find him, but a sharp cry from behind made me turn.

Something skinny and rodent-like bounded towards me

on spindly legs. Its tongue flicked hungrily over two sharp teeth and its beady eyes glistened in the darkness.

Back in my world I had unique abilities – abilities that would make dealing with a creature like this child's play. I could conjure up a machine gun, or a chainsaw, or simply imagine the thing out of existence. I could do all that back there. Here I was powerless.

But I was too angry to care.

The rodent pounced and I was ready for it. I ducked to the side and made a grab for a rock on the ground. As the monster rounded on me I drove the grapefruit-sized stone against the side of its head. It went down with a squeal, and the rage that had brought me here tightened its grip round my chest.

I brought the rock down once more on the creature's head. It squealed again. I kept going, kept hitting until the monster fell silent. My breath came in unsteady gulps as I stood there, staring down at the dead thing in the dirt. My eyes crept to my hand, and to the blood-soaked rock it held.

I looked down once more at the creature and told myself I'd had no option. It or me. That had been the only choice.

I dropped the rock. I turned away. And I saw my dad.

He was standing in a sliver of moonlight just twenty metres away. Close enough for me to see the grin on his face. Had he been smiling when he killed my mum? That was something for me to ask him when I was choking the life from his body.

'Good work, kiddo,' he called over. 'I always said I'd make a killer out of you some day.'

I ran at him, no thought in my head but the need for revenge. No emotions left inside me but hatred and rage. His smile broadened, and I loathed him even more.

'Not so fast,' he said, and the darkness around me shifted as if alive. Something snaked across my path and snagged my feet. I fell hard, clattering against the cracked tarmac and rolling to a stop.

Shapes emerged from the shadows on all sides of me. Monstrous figures and grotesque, deformed faces loomed down. The things in the darkness all looked different. There was nothing to link them to one another, aside from the hatred that burned in their eyes.

I tried to get up, but whatever had tripped me now held my feet together, keeping me from moving.

Shoes scuffed on the road. I looked up and saw my dad stop beside me. He was still smiling as he shook his head and made a soft *tutting* noise below his breath.

'Too easy,' he said. 'You'll never get to me like that.'

'Kill you,' I said, half sobbing. 'I'll kill you.'

He looked at the circle of freaks surrounding us. 'Hear that?' he said. 'My boy's going to kill me.'

The figures began to snuffle and snort with laughter. Someone behind me let out a high-pitched giggle. A memory of hearing it before stirred at the back of my head, but then was gone.

My dad looked down at me again. 'You're not going to kill me, kiddo. You can't kill me. At least,' he gestured around him, 'not here.'

His knees *cricked* as he squatted down beside my head.

He stroked my hair. I pushed his hands away and the night was filled with that laughter again.

'It's been a long road, son,' he said. 'You've worked hard, but it's almost over. You're almost done. The barrier between this world and yours is almost gone. One more big push should do it. One more big push and your world is replaced by this one.'

He straightened up. 'But you can't push it from here. You need to go back there. Use those abilities of yours. Do something spectacular. And then it'll all be over.'

I gritted my teeth. 'I'm not going anywhere.'

His smile widened further until it was nothing but teeth. 'Wrong,' he said, then he drew back his foot and a jolt of pain snapped back my head.

'Come on. Come on, wake up!'

My body and brain roused together. There were hands on my shoulders. I lunged forward, brushing them off and grabbing for whoever had touched me.

My hands found Billy's windpipe and forced him

backwards into the snow. Billy had been the hardest boy in my school once upon a time. Back when I'd been trying to stop Caddie and Raggy Maggie, he'd even stuck a knife into my stomach.

And now here he was, pinned beneath me, his eyes shimmering with panic, his breath stuck halfway down his throat. My hands twitched. I could squeeze, pay him back for the years of misery he'd inflicted on me. I could squeeze, and I could keep squeezing.

But Billy had changed. Or maybe Billy had stayed the same, and I was the one who was different. Whatever, he wasn't a threat to anyone any more. He'd helped stop the Beast. Impossible as it seemed, he and I were on the same side these days.

I relaxed my grip, then removed my hands from his throat. 'Sorry,' I said, my voice hoarse. He gave a bug-eyed nod in return and gingerly rubbed his throat.

'Don't worry about it,' he croaked, and we helped each other up out of the snow.

The body of the Beast still lay motionless on the ground,

its blood pinkening the snow around it. I forced myself to think of it in those terms – an "it", a "thing", because the reality was too terrible to consider. I didn't want to remember what – or rather *who* – the Beast had once been.

But it had saved me, and that told me the person it once was had still been in there somewhere, buried deep down beneath the scales and the claws and the slavering jaws.

The other beast, the one that had started the whole nightmare off, was nowhere to be seen. We'd killed it, the three of us together – Billy, Ameena and me – but now it was gone. It was no great surprise. I'd learned from Mr Mumbles that if you killed anything from the Darkest Corners when it was in the real world, it was reborn back over there.

That monster still lived, but there was no coming back for the one who had saved us all.

Ameena was sitting in the snow, staring at nothing, her head shaking ever so slightly left to right. She'd discovered she wasn't real, that every memory she had was false. She was "a tool", my dad had said. A tool my terrified mind had created to save me from Mr Mumbles. With just a few choice words, he'd shown her that her entire life was a lie.

I stood over her, no idea what to say. What *could* I say? How could you help someone who didn't really exist? In the end, I said the only thing that came into my head.

'Hey.'

She blinked, as if wakening from a dream. Her head stopped shaking and tilted just a little. Her dark eyes peered up at me from behind a curtain of darker hair. She breathed out a cloud of misty white vapour.

'Hey.'

'You OK?'

She shook her head again. 'Not great. You?'

I shrugged. There was a throbbing in my jaw where my dad had kicked me. Another addition to go along with all the other aches and pains throughout my body. 'Been better.'

A piercing scream came from the direction of the police station. The screechers – the zombie-like things that had once been the people from my village – had been driven back by the battle of the Beasts. Now they emerged cautiously from streets and alleyways on all sides, their black eyes gazing hungrily upon us.

'Screechers,' Billy whispered.

'I know,' I said. 'I see them.'

They were at various stages of mutation. At first we'd thought they were all just zombies. Then we'd discovered that this was just the first stage in a transformation that would eventually see them become like the Beast itself.

Some of those that moved to surround us now were still shuffling on two legs. Others crawled through the snow, their shapes barely recognisable as human.

'What do we do?' Billy asked.

'I don't know.'

I could feel Billy glaring at me. 'You don't know? What do you mean you don't know?'

'I don't know, Billy.' I squeezed the bridge of my nose,

trying to ease the headache that spread out from there. 'It's been a bit of a rough day.'

'Well, it's going to get rougher if we don't do something,' he pointed out. He looked around at the screechers. They were still approaching slowly, eyeing the fallen Beast, not yet realising it was dead. The moment they did, there would be nothing to hold them back.

I turned to Billy. 'And what should we do?' I asked him. 'Because I'm open to suggestions here.'

'We run,' Billy said. 'We can run.'

'Run where, exactly?'

'The church,' he said quickly. 'We can hide in the church.'

I shook my head. 'No, we can't. It's full of screechers. They'd—

Billy pushed past me, panic flashing across his face. He made a dive for Ameena, but she was too fast. I turned to see her sprinting away, running straight for the closest group of screechers.

'Ameena, stop!' I cried, but she didn't slow. The

screechers ahead of her began lumbering more quickly, teeth gnashing as they staggered forward to intercept her.

'What's she doing?' he asked. 'Is she trying to get herself killed or something?'

The realisation hit like a hammer blow. 'Oh, God,' I whispered. 'She is. That's exactly what she's trying to do.'

Taking their cue from the others, the rest of the screechers began to pick up the pace. Their screams and howls filled the air as they began shambling and leaping and bounding towards us and towards Ameena.

I heard Billy whimper. 'We're going to die. We're going to die!'

'We can't die,' I said. 'If we die, then he gets away with it. He gets away with killing my mum.'

A jolt of electricity buzzed through my scalp. I knew that using my abilities was playing right into my dad's hands, but what choice did I have? If I died, he got away with it.

And there was no way he was getting away with it.

I closed my eyes. The blue sparks I saw whenever I

used my abilities shimmered behind my eyelids as I raised both hands and let my imagination take over.

There was a *whumpf* as a circle of snow swirled up into a blizzard around us. It hit the screechers like a solid wall, battering them back, buying us some time.

Ameena stopped running. She didn't turn to look at us, just sank down on to her knees and stared straight ahead. I set off towards her, pulling Billy behind me.

'Come on, help me get her,' I said. 'We'll take her to the church.'

'I thought you said it was full of screechers?'

'It is,' I said, and the sparks flickered behind my eyes. 'But leave that to me.'

Chapter Two

POWER STRUGGLE

We ran for the church, Ameena held between us. She stumbled along, keeping pace, but I knew if we let go of her she'd stop and fall.

The screechers were on the move again, thundering through the snow after us. Billy and I dragged Ameena up the stone steps and in through the heavy double doors. We fell inside and I closed the doors again with a slam.

We could hear the screams and the howls of the screechers inside the church. I nudged open the inner door that led through to the top of the aisle. The screams were coming from the little side room behind the pulpit, where I'd led the screechers when they were chasing me down.

'Wait here,' I said. Ignoring Billy's protests, I stepped into the main church and made my way towards the pulpit. A towering statue of Jesus on the cross stood by the entrance to the side room. I spared it just a glance as I strode closer to the open door.

Halfway down the aisle I stopped. 'Hey!' I shouted, and my voice bounced back at me from the high ceiling. The screeches within the side room changed in tone. I heard a frantic clattering, and through they came.

They had entered the church mostly human, but now they were mostly beast. Two or three still stood upright, but their backs were bent and their shoulders were stooped, and jagged outcrops of bone tore up through their thickening skin.

Half a dozen more were on all fours, their bodies twisted and buckled, their limbs and necks broadening and stretching almost before my eyes.

There were no lingering hungry glares from any of them this time. They had no reason to hold back. They collided with each other in their hurry to get to me, and in a split second, the fastest and strongest was hurtling along the aisle towards me.

It had been a man, I guessed, although I couldn't say why. There was something vaguely male about the scraps of humanity it had left, but then that may just have been my imagination.

It bounded like a big cat along the aisle, its glossy black eyes trained on my throat. It wanted to kill me, this thing. It wanted to open my neck, spill my blood across the floor. It wanted me dead.

But I could not die. If I died, he got away with it.

I raised a hand, felt the sparks flash. When I clenched my fist, something inside the screecher went *krik*. Blood burst on its lips as it let out a pained yelp. The next bound was its last. It slid to a stop at my feet, and it didn't move again.

My eyes raised to the next screecher. It didn't hesitate as it closed in for the kill – but neither did I. With a single gesture I hurled it backwards into the others. The sparks crackled like lightning inside my head. My hands moved like a conductor leading an orchestra and, one by one, the screechers fell.

In seconds there was only the echo of their screams around the church, and then there wasn't even that.

The door behind me opened with a creak. I heard Billy draw in a sharp breath.

'What... what have you done?'

'Someone had to,' I said, not looking round. 'Someone had to stop them or we'd all have been dead.'

'But they were people,' Billy protested.

'*Were*. Past tense.' I turned to face him. He led Ameena in by the arm. 'And how come you care anyway? You were all "destroy the brain" earlier. What made you start giving a damn?'

He looked me up and down. 'What made you stop?'

'Whoa.' Ameena was staring down at the screecher by my feet. She shrugged free of Billy and took a few tentative steps towards it. 'It looks dead. Is it dead?'

'It's dead.'

'He killed it,' Billy said.

Ameena's eyes met mine. She cocked her head to the side a little. 'You killed it?'

'I killed it.' She kept looking at me. 'It would've killed us,' I felt compelled to add.

'Yeah,' she said at last. 'I suppose it would at that.'

'How do you feel now?' I asked her.

'This is the church,' she said, ignoring the question. 'Where you blew up the donkey.'

Billy frowned. 'You *blew* up a donkey? What, like...?' He formed a pea-shooter shape with his hand, raised it to his mouth and puffed out his cheeks.

'What? No, I didn't *blow up* a donkey,' I said. 'I blew a donkey *up*. As in exploded it.'

Billy lowered his hand. 'Oh. Right. Why did you do that then?'

'It wasn't a real donkey. It was concrete.'

'Right,' said Billy. He thought about this. 'I still come back to "Why did you do that then?".'

'Forget it. Doesn't matter.' I turned back to Ameena. 'You should sit down.'

'I don't need to sit down,' she said, then she sat down anyway. 'I'm... fine. I think.' She looked at me with hopeful eyes. 'Am I?'

I gave a nod. 'He could've been lying,' I said. 'He was probably lying. He does that. He—

'He wasn't lying,' she said. 'It was true. Everything he said – it was true. I can see that now. Before I found you fighting Mr Mumbles... there's nothing. I don't remember anything. Not properly anyway, just... images, like photos someone's shown me.' She shrugged and shook her head. 'Hell, I don't even know my last name. But then that's because I haven't got one. Because you never gave me one.'

I suddenly felt guilty for that. 'Sorry.'

'Don't worry about it. You were being murdered by a maniac,' Ameena said. She jumped up and clapped me on the shoulder. 'That sort of thing can be distracting.'

She gave her arms a shake and kicked out her legs, and with that, the tension seemed to leave her. 'So,' she said, cracking her knuckles. 'I've changed my mind on the whole killing-myself thing. Sorry about that. Such a drama queen sometimes.'

'No problem,' I said.

'Good. Now what's the plan?'

'I find my dad,' I said. 'And then I kill him.'

She nodded slowly. 'OK, well that's a plan. That's definitely a plan.'

'What about them?' Billy asked. He pointed back towards the door. 'What about them out there?'

'They're not my problem,' I said.

'And what about us?' Billy asked. 'Are we not your problem either? Look, I know you're angry at your dad.'

'Angry?' I said. '*Angry?* He killed my mum, Billy. Don't you get it? He— The words caught in my throat. My eyes went hot and the room began to spin. I reached for a pew to support myself, but missed and dropped to my knees on the hard floor.

'He killed my mum,' I croaked as tears rolled like raindrops down my cheeks. 'He killed my mum.'

A bubble welled up inside me. It tightened my chest

and pushed down on my stomach. I tried to speak again, but the pressure inside me made it impossible.

Ameena knelt beside me. Without a word, she wrapped her arms round my shoulders and pulled me in close. We sat there rocking back and forth, my tears coming in big silent sobs.

When the tears finally stopped I just sat there, feeling nothing but empty. But then even that moment passed. I pulled away from Ameena, unable to look at her, and stood up.

Billy cleared his throat. 'You OK?'

I nodded quickly to hide my embarrassment. 'Fine.'

Ameena got to her feet and I realised she had a smear of my snot on her shoulder. I couldn't quite bring myself to tell her.

'So, what are we going to do?' Billy asked.

'I told you. I'm going to find my dad and then I'm going to kill him,' I said.

'Right. So we're sticking with that one then, are we?' he asked. 'You know you're playing right into his hands, don't you? He wants you to do your... magic, or whatever.'

'Well,' I said. 'Looks like he's going to get what he wants.'

'Then he wins,' Billy said. 'And you're right, he does get what he wants. Whatever he's done to you – your mum, your nan – he did it all to make you do what he wants. He's manipulating you, and you're going to let him.'

'Check out the voice of reason,' said Ameena.

'I'm right, though. If you keep doing your thing then the barrier breaks down and suddenly we're up to our eyes in monsters.'

'We're already up to our eyes in monsters,' I reminded him.

'Yeah,' Billy conceded. 'But you and I both know there are worse things waiting over there. We've seen them. If they get through, they'll kill everyone.'

'Everyone important is already dead.'

A *thud* against the front doors cut the argument short.

A muffled screech filled the church. A few seconds later there was a chorus of them howling out there as they hammered and pounded against the doors.

'They're going to get inside,' Ameena said. She released Billy and he stumbled out of her reach, nursing his arm. 'Decision time, kiddo. What's it to be?'

The sounds of the screechers seemed to be inside the church now. I could almost picture them, their deformed heads forcing their way through the splintering wood, their teeth chewing hungrily at the air. It was Billy who made a decision.

'Help me block these,' he said, hurrying along the aisle to the inner swing doors. 'It'll buy us some time.'

Ameena looked to me. I nodded, and she headed off after Billy. There were two large tables by the doors, one stacked upside down atop the other. They grabbed each end of the top table and began moving into position in front of the doors.

They were right in front of the doors when they began to open. Teeth flashed in the gap. Billy and Ameena leapt back. A hundred thousand sparks filled my head and an invisible force pushed the door closed.

'Stand back,' I told them, and they darted over to join me. The table moved with just a thought from me. It tilted and fell so the top was up against the doors, which I was still holding closed.

Next I pictured the back pews sliding across the floor. The metal bolts holding them in place groaned, then snapped. I felt my brain tingle as the heavy wooden benches fell into place behind the table. Only then did I let the sparks fade away.

The doors swung inward a few centimetres then hit the barricade with a loud *thud*. Screeches of frustration came at us through the wood, but the barrier held steady for the moment.

'Nice work,' Ameena said. 'That was close.'

'Uh, guys.' Billy's voice was a low whisper. I turned to find him nodding at a spot several metres behind me.

Something stood there. Or rather, something flickered there. It was faint, like the outline of a ghost. A large ghost, with too many limbs. We watched it pacing towards us, then it faded away completely.

'OK,' Ameena muttered. 'So what the Hell was that?'

I turned, casting my gaze around the dimly lit church. There were half a dozen or more figures dotted about, half appearing and fading before my eyes. I recognised some of them as the things that had surrounded me in the Darkest Corners.

'It's happening,' I realised. 'Like he said. The barrier's weakening. They're going to come through.'

'Not necessarily,' Billy said, although he didn't sound convinced. 'I mean, you can just stop, right? If you don't do your mojo any more, they can't come any further.' He glanced from me to Ameena and back and swallowed nervously. 'Right?'

'Yeah,' I said, but the doubt in my voice was obvious. 'If I don't do anything else, the barrier will stay standing.'

A soft hissing and crackling noise began to echo around the church. I looked up to the source of the sound and saw a speaker mounted high on the wall behind the pulpit.

The next sound I heard made my skin crawl.

Fiona, it's time to get up now.

That was my dad's voice. My dad's voice from the recording he had played me earlier.

'No,' I said softly. 'N-no, please.'

The hospital machines *beeped* on the soundtrack. I heard my mum rouse and my dad smile. Even on the tape, I heard him smile.

That's my girl. Open your eyes now. Open your...

My mum gave a groan. Ameena reached for me, but I pulled away. I stared at the speaker, and I stared, and I stared.

Wh-where am I? My mum's voice, shaky and weak.

Look at me, Fiona. Look at me.

On the tape, my mum gave a gasp. 'No,' I whispered. 'Don't.'

As if echoing me, she cried out, and I could hear all the fear and the panic in her voice. I raised my hands, stabbing them towards the speaker. *N-no. Please, no, don—*

'Kyle, no!' Billy cried.

'Do it,' Ameena urged. 'Shut it up.'

BANG!

The speaker exploded before the gunshot had a chance to ring. Before he had a chance to kill her again. The sparks buzzed across my head, then receded again, leaving only the charred remains of the speaker behind.

'What did you do?' Billy groaned. 'What have you done?'

'Leave it, Billy,' Ameena said, and this time I let her press her hand against my shoulder.

A sudden fluttering up by the rafters made us all jump. A small black shape flapped around at the ceiling. We followed its flight until it landed on one of Christ's outstretched arms. A beady black eye gazed blankly down at us.

Billy let out a nervous laugh. 'God, that nearly gave me a heart attack,' he breathed. 'Just a bird.'

'Not just a bird,' I said, trying to keep my voice low

and controlled. Ameena and I both stepped back, our eyes never leaving those of the bird. 'It's a crow.'

Billy shrugged. 'So? What's so bad about crows?'

'Obviously you've never met the ones we've met,' Ameena told him.

And he hadn't. He hadn't been there at Marion's house when the Crowmaster attacked. He hadn't seen Marion's skeletal remains, the skin, muscle and sinew torn off by a murder of flesh-eating crows.

But I had seen it. And it was something I'd never be able to forget.

'He's dead, isn't he?' Ameena whispered.

'No,' I said. 'He died here in the real world. That means he was reborn over there.'

'Oh, now that's just cheating,' she protested.

'No argument there,' I said. The bird wasn't moving, just watching us in silence. 'I couldn't agree more.'

'What's the problem?' Billy asked. 'However mean and scary you say it is, it's just one bird.'

The cries of the screechers were louder than ever. The table and pews groaned against the floor as they were pushed back.

'No,' I said quietly. 'It's never just one bird.'

And then, in a heaving torrent of squawking black, the space inside the church was torn in two.

Chapter Three

THE TOWER

We ran for cover as the crows came. They surged in their hundreds through a hole in reality itself, filling the church with the thunder of their wings.

Ameena pulled me down behind a pew as Billy took cover behind the one across the aisle. The crows were a dark tornado around us, squawking and cawing as they circled the inside of the church.

A figure stepped through the cloud of birds, short and stocky, his face hidden beneath a rough brown sack. Back at Marion's house the Crowmaster had been revealed as nothing more than a little man called Joe Crow, who liked to dress in a scarecrow costume. The costume was gone now, but Joe was doing everything he could to maintain the Crowmaster act.

'I see you, boy,' he said. His voice was still like fingernails down a blackboard. The tattered eyeholes in the sack turned in my direction. I raised my head to reply, but a crow swooped down at me, forcing me to duck again. 'You thought you'd seen the last of the Crowmaster,' he said, and then there was that laugh of his again, audible even over the screechers and the birds: *SS-SS-SS-SS*. 'You thought that your nightmares was over, but, boy, they's just beginning.'

'Shut him up,' Ameena said.

'How?'

She glanced along at the barricaded doors. It took me a moment to realise what she meant. Her eyes drilled into me, urging me on. Along the aisle, Joe Crow paced towards us on his tiny legs.

I nodded. The sparks lit up the inside of my head and the doors flew open. Joe Crow stopped advancing as the screechers burst through. Their eyes locked on him. Their jaws gnashed.

'Aw,' Joe groaned, 'crap.'

They were on him before his birds could react, ripping and tearing at him, their teeth already slick with blood.

His command over them broken, the birds began to thud against the walls and fall to the floor. I moved to run for the door, but there were more screechers rushing through.

Ameena and I began clambering quickly over the pews in front, and Billy raced to do the same. The screechers were still busy with Joe Crow, and we hurdled our way to the front without them noticing us. Together, all three of us ran for the back room and hurriedly closed the door.

'This way,' I said, making for the rear exit that led out into the graveyard. As I pulled it open a hand clawed through the gap. Billy and Ameena rushed over and threw their weight against the wood. Between us, we forced the door closed, but the screecher on the other side was already trying to break it down.

'What now?' Billy yelped.

'Magic them away,' Ameena told me. 'If you're ever going to do your thing, now's the time.'

'Don't be stupid,' Billy told her. 'You saw what happened. Those things are starting to come through.'

'So what do we do, Billy? Just wait here to die?'

'What's it matter to you?' Billy asked her, and I could see his old wicked streak shining through. 'It's not like you were ever alive to begin with.'

'Ladder,' I said, pushing between them. A metal ladder was attached to one of the walls. It led straight up to a hatch in the high ceiling. 'It must lead to the tower. We can hide there.'

'For how long?' Ameena asked. 'Up there we'll have nowhere to run to.'

A clawed hand punched a hole through the back door. There was no more time to make plans.

'Go,' I said, gesturing for Ameena to lead the way up the ladder. She hesitated, but then set off at a breakneck rate. By the time Billy was halfway up, she was already at the top, pushing open the hatch and clambering through.

I went last. When I got to the top, Billy reached down and helped pull me up into the tower. The hatch closed over just as the back door came down, and we heard the screecher howl in confusion.

'We're safe,' I whispered.

'Maybe for now,' Ameena added quietly.

The inside of the tower was dark and gloomy. There had once been a bell up there, but it had long since been removed. The rectangular openings in each wall that would once have allowed the chimes to ring out across the village were boarded over, letting only scraps of light seep through. The floor was thick with dust. Mousetraps were dotted here and there around the little square room. Billy kicked one to the side and it snapped shut with a *clack*.

'Sssh!' I hissed. I pointed down at the floor, and to the screecher that lurked below.

'That's our plan then, is it?' Ameena asked. 'We stay up here and keep quiet?'

'You got any better ideas?' I asked.

'What happened to finding your dad? When did that plan stop?'

Billy answered for me. 'When he realised he was playing right into his dad's hands.'

'We don't know that's true,' Ameena protested. 'Kyle, if you want to get him for what he did, you're going to have to use your abilities. That's just how it is.'

Billy looked Ameena up and down. 'Why are you so determined he should go all Harry Potter all of a sudden? How come you're acting so weird?'

Ameena bit her lip. 'What can I say?' she muttered. 'It's been a weird day.'

Weird day? That was an understatement if ever I'd heard one. It had been a weird month. The weirdest, *worst* month of my life. Possibly of anyone's life ever. And even that wasn't doing it justice.

'I don't know what to do,' I admitted. 'Everything's broken. I've... I've ruined everything. '

Ameena rolled her eyes. 'And I thought *I* was being a drama queen! You haven't ruined anything, kiddo. Your dad has. All you've done is try to stay alive and try to protect people.'

I looked her in the eye. 'That's not working out too well, is it?'

My lip wobbled and I looked away again. My mum: dead. My nan: dead. My mum's cousin Marion: dead. So much for protecting people.

And then there was Joseph, the mystery man. He'd popped up all over the place with his cryptic clues, helping me when I didn't even know it. I'd watched him die too, right before my eyes, and I still didn't know who he was.

'We sit tight,' Billy said. 'That's the plan. We sit here and wait for help to arrive.'

'Help isn't going to arrive, Billy. Grow up,' Ameena said.

'How do you know?'

'Because this isn't a bedtime story. There's no knight in shining armour climbing up this tower. There's no fairy godmother about to come swooping in. There's just us.' She pointed to the boarded-up window. 'And there's just them. If we want to live we have to fight. That's how it is.'

Ameena turned to me. 'And you're the best fighter we've got. Much as I hate to admit it.'

Billy shook his head. 'You're not buying this, are you? You saw what was happening down there. I don't want more monsters coming through.'

'What's the matter, Billy? Scared?'

'Of course I'm scared!' Billy yelped. 'I'm terrified. I've never been more scared in my whole life, and if he starts doing his, his *thing*, then it's all just going to get worse.'

Ameena spun to face him. 'You don't get it, do you? This is it. This is the end. It can't *get* any worse.'

'Don't say that,' I groaned. 'As soon as anyone says "It can't get any worse," it always gets worse.'

'Not this time,' Ameena said, turning back to face me. 'Everyone in this village has been turned into a monster, and they're going to spread like a virus all over the planet. Your mum is dead. Your dad is out there somewhere, waiting to unleash God knows what on the world, and we're stuck in an attic with a screecher downstairs and Billy No-Dates for company.'

'Maybe... maybe someone will come,' I said weakly.

'*No one's coming!*' Ameena said. 'There's no one to fix this but us. But *you.*'

'Why are you doing this?' Billy snapped. 'Why do you keep egging him on? It's like you *want* him to break down this big barrier thing.' He looked to me. 'She's pushing you into it.'

'Don't be stupid, Billy,' I said. 'Of course she isn't.'

'How can you be so sure?' Billy asked. 'You said yourself you don't know anything about her. How do you know she's not working with your dad?'

Ameena drove her elbow into Billy's face. He staggered back, his hands over his nose, a sharp yelp of pain bursting on his lips.

'*Whoa!* What did you do that for?' I asked. I was used to sudden bouts of violence from Ameena, but never like that.

'You heard him.' Ameena sounded defensive. 'He was starting to rant. Ranting's noisy, and the last thing we want right now is someone getting noisy.' She smiled in that way that made her nose wrinkle up. 'Am I right, kiddo? Course I am; I'm always right.'

I began to smile, then stopped. That word replayed in my head.

'Kiddo,' I said, my face fixed in a half-smile. 'You called me "kiddo".'

'Yeah? So? I always call you "kiddo", kiddo. It's one of the things that makes me so adorable.'

A sickening stirring began in my gut. I glanced at Billy, who was still clutching his nose. He watched us in silence through eyes filled with tears.

'*He* calls me "kiddo",' I mumbled, and I saw the smile fade from her face. 'My dad calls me "kiddo".'

She shrugged, but it looked forced and not at all natural. 'Does he?' she said. 'What are the chances?'

I stared into her eyes, and in that moment I realised that I didn't really know her at all.

Shadows moved behind her and the sound of in-rushing air filled the tower. The shadows became a man and the man became my dad. He wrapped his arms round Ameena and flashed me a wide grin.

'Whoops,' he sniggered, and then they were gone. I

looked blankly at the spot where Ameena had stood. I was still looking at it when Billy spoke.

'She's gone.'

'He took her,' I said.

The floorboard creaked behind me.

'No,' Billy said. 'They went together.'

'No,' I snapped, turning on him. 'She wouldn't. She's... I...' I curled my fingers into fists. 'Wait here. I'll be back.'

'Back? What do you mean you'll be back? Where are you going?'

But Billy's voice was already becoming distant as I focused on one of the sparks and flitted myself through to the Darkest Corners.

The inside of the tower looked exactly the same, only now the hatch was open. The howls of the screechers had faded along with Billy's voice, but now I could hear a steady *creaking* coming up through the hole in the floor.

I looked down in time to see Ameena jump the last few rungs and land lightly beside my dad. She raised her head and her eyes briefly met mine, then she was off and running with him through the door that led into the main part of the church.

My stomach flipped. I thought back to the figure in the brown hood I'd seen so many times with my dad. Ameena's height. Ameena's build. But it couldn't have been her. I refused to accept it.

She had saved me. So many times, she had saved me. She couldn't have been working with him this whole time. She couldn't.

I called her name, hoping she would come running back to tell me it was all some stupid mistake. To tell me I was wrong, and that she'd never betray me. But she didn't come back. No one came back.

The ladder was more rusted on the way down than it had been on the way up, but that was the Darkest Corners for you. It twisted things, corrupted them. Had it done the same to Ameena somehow? Made her as much a monster as the rest of them? No. No way.

Please no.

I jumped the last few rungs just as she had done and charged through into the main church. It now stood in ruins, most of the sky visible through the crumbled roof. The doors at the far end of the room were still standing. They swung closed as I raced towards them.

A ragged shape lay there in the middle of the aisle. As I drew closer I recognised the tattered remains of Joe Crow. They squirmed as if alive, and I saw his body begin to reform, like footage of rotting fruit played in high-speed reverse.

'S-see you, boy,' he slurred. A half-formed hand reached out for me. 'Don't you g-go nowhere.'

I clambered over the pews beside him, not daring to get too close. The rest of the aisle passed in a blur as I raced through the inner doors and out through the exit into the world beyond.

A foot stuck out from round the doorframe and I tripped. My momentum carried me down the stone steps and I landed on my back on the damp, dirty ground.

My dad stood at the top of the steps, laughing as he

looked down. And there, beside him, was Ameena. My dad and Ameena. Together.

There had been a little hope inside me, buried deep down. A hope that somehow everything was going to be OK. A hope that, no matter how bad things seemed at the moment, they weren't broken beyond repair.

That hope died when I saw them standing there together. My dad was grinning, but I didn't look at him. Instead I just stared at Ameena and asked her, 'Why?'

She shrugged and pushed her hair out of her face. 'Nothing personal.'

'Nothing personal?' I said. I was on my feet in an instant. *'Nothing personal*; are you nuts?'

I began to climb the stairs towards them. Ameena raised her fists and bounced on to the balls of her feet. 'Don't,' she warned.

I stopped. Not because I was scared of her, but because I suddenly had no energy left to climb with.

'So, what?' I asked croakily. 'The whole time? It's all been a lie?'

'Bingo,' laughed my dad. 'All that stuff about you making her, about her being –' he made quotation marks in the air with his fingers – '"a tool"? All rubbish. None of that was true.'

'Then why say it?' I asked. 'What was the point?'

'The point was what it's always been,' he continued. 'To make you care about her. To make you want to protect her.' His grin widened. 'And you do, don't you, kiddo? You care about her *a lot*.'

I didn't answer. Ameena tried to hold my gaze, but glanced away.

'Man, that must be a kick in the teeth,' my dad chuckled. 'There you are falling for her charms, and all the while she's just trying to get you to use your abilities so you break down the barrier and she can get the Hell away from you.'

'It was you in that brown robe all along,' I said. 'It was you.'

'*Bzzzzt!* Correct answer,' cried my dad. 'And I think if you're honest with yourself you always really knew that. You just didn't want to believe it. Am I right? *Kiddo?*'

I didn't answer, just kept staring and waiting for it to sink in. She'd been working against me. Right from day one, she'd been working against me.

My dad put a finger behind his ear and pushed it slightly forward. 'You know, the walls between this world and yours must be paper-thin now. If you listen, you can hear your little friend Billy screaming.'

He was right. Billy's screams were muffled, but there was no mistaking them. They came from high up in the church, a whole other world away. They were screams not of panic, but of pain.

My dad and Ameena stepped apart, leaving the path to the door clear. 'You've got maybe a minute to get back there and save him,' said my dad. 'Or you can stay here and chitchat with us. The choice is yours.'

Far away, Billy let out a squeal of agony. My dad's face lit up with a manic grin.

'But whatever you decide, you'd better do it quickly.'

Chapter Four

FAMILIAR FACES

I threw the church doors open and sprinted along the aisle. I was still in the Darkest Corners – it was too dangerous to jump back into my own world until I was up the ladder and inside the tower itself – and Joe Crow had almost finished pulling himself back together on the ruined church floor.

He was drawing himself up on his stubby legs as I ran towards him. The sackcloth mask he had been wearing hadn't made the trip back with him, and his wrinkled, old-man face twisted into a scowl at my approach. He snarled, revealing dozens of tiny, shark-like teeth poking out from his pale gums.

'I see you came back, boy,' he spat; then he stopped

talking as the sole of my shoe slammed hard into the centre of his weather-beaten face. He stumbled backwards on to the floor, and then I was past him, through the door behind the pulpit and scrabbling up the rusted ladder.

I was halfway up before I realised I couldn't hear Billy screaming, and all the way at the top before I realised I couldn't hear anything from within the tower at all.

As soon as I was through the hatch I focused on a spark and moved between worlds. To my relief, Billy was there, almost exactly where I'd left him. He was kneeling down, facing away from me, his hands hanging limply by his sides so his knuckles were almost touching the floor.

He was half hidden by the shadows, but as I took a step closer I saw the spots of blood on the side of his face. I thought back. He hadn't been bleeding after Ameena hit him, had he? In all the panic, I couldn't remember.

'Are you OK?' I asked. 'What happened?'

Billy didn't answer. Up close I could see that his whole body was vibrating. His breath was whistling unsteadily in and out, and he gave the occasional soft whimper as I took another creaky step closer.

'I heard you screaming,' I said. He flinched, but didn't turn round. I took another step towards him. 'What happened? Why were you screaming?'

Billy's trembling was becoming more and more violent, as if his body was going deep into shock. He flinched again as I laid my hand on his shoulder.

'What's wrong, Billy?' I asked. 'What happened? Talk to me.'

With a sob, he slowly turned his head. I felt my guts twist in horror. I stumbled away from him, swallowing the urge to throw up. His eyes bored into mine, ringed with red and filled with tears.

I tried to speak, but no words came. Tried to scream, but my throat was closed tight. Instead I raised a shaking hand and pointed. Pointed at his face; at his mouth; at the thick black stitches that threaded through his lips, pulling them tightly together.

He tried to say something, but the words came out as

a jumbled mumble of syllables. His fingers brushed against the stitches, then pulled quickly away. His eyes bulged. His nostrils flared. He let out a high-pitched moan that would have been a scream if he could open his mouth.

'Wh-who...?' I began, but a blast of music answered my question before I could even ask it.

It came from the room below, loud enough to shake the floor beneath us.

If you go down to the woods today, you're in for a big surprise...

'No,' I whispered. 'Not him. Not here.'

If you go down to the woods today, you'd better go in disguise...

Of all the fiends I'd faced so far, Doc Mortis was up there with the worst of them. He was a sadist, a madman who believed himself to be a surgeon, and who kidnapped innocent people and performed grotesque operations on them. I'd barely escaped his hospital. I thought he was dead. It appeared I was wrong.

A *crash* of breaking wood temporarily drowned out the music from below. One of the wooden boards that had been fastened over an opening in the tower wall was smashed in right behind Billy.

Before he could even turn, a freakishly thin figure reached through the gap. I caught a glimpse of its bald head and its surgical mask. Eyes that were no more than buttons stitched on to skin flashed at me through the gloom, and I recognised one of Doc's porters.

A scarred hand caught Billy by the back of his jacket and dragged him towards the hole in the wall.

Today's the day the teddy bears have their picnic...

'Billy!' I cried, reaching out a hand. His fingertips touched mine, but then he was gone, dragged out into the chill night air. I ran to the broken wood and looked out. Screechers heaved through the streets, but there was no sign of Billy or the porter anywhere. They couldn't have gone far, though. I had to find him. Too many people had suffered because of me as it was.

The wind pushed against me as I squeezed out through

the gap and on to the roof, which led down at a steep angle from the side of the tower. The roof extended a few centimetres past the top of the wall, and beyond that lay a dizzyingly long drop to the ground.

With great care I inched away from the tower, trying to get a better view of the roof. My feet slipped on the snow-covered slates and I had to grab for the broken board to stop me sliding off.

My legs kicked frantically, trying to back-pedal to safety. I dug in my heels and pushed until I was finally able to get back into a standing position.

I spent a few seconds getting my nerves back under control, then looked around for Billy. Aside from mine, there were no footprints in the snow. I craned my neck and looked at the top of the tower, but nothing moved up there in the dark.

'Billy,' I hissed. 'Where are you?' But only the wind replied.

Dozens of panicked screeches began to rise up from below. I leaned out, trying to see over the edge and down to the street. I held on to the wood with my fingertips, craning my neck in an attempt to—

Something slammed against my fingers from inside the tower. There was no time to turn and see who or what was responsible. My feet slipped out from under me and I began to slide towards the edge of the roof.

The sparks fizzled behind my eyes, and I had to grit my teeth and force myself not to give in. Billy had been right. Using my abilities was playing right into my dad's hands. Was playing right into *Ameena's* hands. He – *they* – were trying to make me end the world. He'd told me right from the start I was going to kill everyone on Earth. I wasn't going to let him be right.

I closed my eyes and let myself go limp. It was the best I could come up with at short notice.

The edge of the roof came up quickly, the ground almost as fast. The snow was thin beside the wall, the church sheltering that spot from the worst of the snowfall. I landed with a *crunch* on icy gravel. The impact forced a yelp from me and a dozen deformed figures turned to look in my direction.

I climbed clumsily to my feet, using the church's brickwork to pull myself into a standing position. A jolt of pain shot up my spine from where I'd hit the ground. I glanced frantically left and right, searching for a way past the screechers, but the screechers were busy with problems of their own.

Something that was more Beast than anything else pounded through the snow on all fours, its huge head lolling left and right. Hot saliva dripped from the monster's mouth, melting the snow where it fell. It advanced slowly on the screechers, then occasionally leapt at them and snapped its vast jaws.

I pressed myself in tight to the wall, half hidden in a narrow alcove. The screechers who had seen me hesitated briefly, but the beast-like thing began to gain on them and their instinct for survival forced them to leave me behind.

I waited, holding my breath until this new Beast had herded the screechers away, then I crept out across the snow and into the street. The darkness was drawing in, and only a few of the streetlights were working. Staring into the gloom, I tried calling Billy's name again – quietly, so as not to attract unwanted attention.

No such luck. A screecher appeared in the doorway of the church. Its black eyes scanned the street. Its nose, now elongated into a narrow snout, snuffled hungrily at the air. Its head snapped in my direction and I began to run, tripping and stumbling through the deep snow.

The house I'd hidden in with Ameena and the others was right ahead. The door was closed, but I knew it was unlocked. The howls of the screecher grew louder behind me as I slipped and skidded along the path. I grabbed for the handle and tumbled inside, kicking the door closed just as the screecher launched itself towards me.

There was a *thud* and the letterbox flapped open. My fingers were too cold and my hands were shaking too badly for me to work the lock. It took four or five attempts before I managed to slide the snib closed. Outside, the screecher gnashed and snarled as it hurled itself against the door.

Turning and running for the stairs, I took them two at

a time until I reached the top. One of the doors on the upper landing was in pieces. The body of the screecher that had once been Billy's cousin lay just beyond it. Gusts of icy wind blew in through the room's broken window.

I picked another door and found myself in a small bathroom. The light switch was outside the room. I flicked it on as I ran past, and slammed the door behind me.

Either the screecher was no longer hammering on the front door, or I was too far away to hear it. I put my ear close to the bathroom door and listened for any sign of the thing.

Nothing. There was only silence in the house.

I crossed to the toilet, closed the lid, and sat down. I had to figure out what to do next. I realised quite quickly that the list of options wasn't long.

With Joseph dead, Billy missing and Ameena working against me, there was no one to help me. For the first time since all this had happened I was truly on my own.

I forced myself to focus on the problems one at a time. All the villagers were mutating into monsters. That was a biggie. More than that, though, the barrier between the real world and the Darkest Corners was almost gone. If I used my abilities again it might collapse completely, letting the horrors of that world flood fully into this one.

Billy was gone, taken to... where? I had no idea. But his stitched-up lips and the sudden appearance of the hospital porter had me convinced that Doc Mortis was not only alive, but somewhere close by.

And then there was Ameena. Ameena, the girl I'd thought of as my best friend, my *only* friend. Ameena, who I thought would always have my back, no matter what horrors we were facing.

Ameena, who had been playing me like an idiot right from the very start.

I bent forward, letting my head rest on my hands. When I thought back, dozens of niggling little doubts swam through my mind. My dad was right, I'd had suspicions about Ameena from early on, but had ignored them because I was too scared to go on without her. Too scared to do anything without her there beside me.

And now she wasn't there. And I was terrified.

So, to recap – everyone I loved was dead; the world was on the brink of disaster, and I was almost certainly to blame; the one person I thought I could trust was now my enemy; and Billy, the enemy who had become a friend, had been snatched away.

Oh, and I was locked in a bathroom with monsters roaming outside. But hey, at least it couldn't get any worse.

I regretted that last thought the moment it popped into my head. What had I said in the tower earlier? It could *always* get worse.

There was a *click* from the hall outside and the light above me went out, plunging the bathroom into darkness. I held my breath and listened for movement outside the door, but the next sound I heard came from right there in the bathroom with me.

It was a giggle, like the one I had recognised earlier. It came from over on my right. I stood up. My eyes were adjusting to the gloom, allowing me to make out a figure standing in the bath, half hidden by a plastic shower curtain.

My throat went dry. Even in the dark, I recognised the outline. Terror cut through me like a knife blade as a voice came in a scratchy sing-song whisper.

'Peek-a-boo. I seeeee you!'

Chapter Five

JUST NOT CRICKET

I didn't dare move, didn't dare breathe, didn't dare tear my eyes away from the small, frail-looking girl who stood in the bath.

Her white, Victorian-style dress was spattered with blood. Her eyes, ringed clumsily with eye shadow, peered out through a curtain of lank hair. A smear of red lipstick bled across her mouth, from one pale cheek to another.

And there, clutched in her hands, was a cracked and dirty porcelain doll, its one remaining eye fixed on me, as if watching for my reaction.

I'd thought the day could not get any worse. But the day had just proved me wrong.

Caddie had once been Billy's imaginary friend. She'd

turned up at my school one day with her doll, Raggy Maggie, and had immediately made my life a living Hell. But I'd eventually beaten her. To the best of my knowledge, she was one of the few fiends I'd fought who was dead. Properly dead. And yet, here she was.

'Raggy Maggie's very cross,' she said, derailing my train of thought. 'You sent us back to the bad place. We told you not to send us back to the bad place, but you didn't listen.'

She raised the doll to her ear and bobbed its head up and down. I could see that aside from the crack it had always had, the doll's head was in one piece. The last time I'd seen it, the head had been broken in two.

'You think we should do *what*, Raggy Maggie?' Caddie asked. Her dark eyes looked me up and down. 'Yes, that would be a fun game, wouldn't it?' She smiled, then kissed the doll on its dirty forehead. 'Oh, Raggy Maggie, you *are* naughty.'

'You're dead,' I said, finally managing to find my voice. 'You're dead. I saw you die.'

Caddie stamped her foot. It made a hollow *thunk* against the plastic bath. 'That is a horrible thing to say,' she said, her bottom lip turned out. She covered the doll's ears with her hands. 'Don't you listen to him, Raggy Maggie. He's *horrible.*'

'You can't really be here.' I pressed a thumb and finger against my eyes, but they were still there when I looked again. 'You're not here,' I insisted. 'You're not real.'

The little girl let out her little giggle. 'Of course we're not real, silly,' she said. Her eyes went to the doll, and she began to swing Raggy Maggie lazily back and forth by her arms. 'None of this is real.'

I hesitated. She hummed a nursery rhyme softly below her breath. A draught came from nowhere and brought goosebumps to the back of my neck.

'What do you mean?'

'Well, of course it isn't real,' she said, her voice and face suddenly solemn. 'Monsters, magic, people with sewing where their mouths are?' She looked sadly at Raggy Maggie. 'Talking dolls? How could any of that be real?'

'But… but it *is* real. All of it. I saw it happen.'

She stopped swinging the doll. 'No, silly, you *dreamed* it happening.'

I blinked, and she was out of the bath, standing right in front of me in high-heeled shoes that were far too large for her feet. 'You're very sick, Kyle. And you're dreaming,' she whispered. With one hand she raised Raggy Maggie until the doll's face was right by mine. Its painted features came alive and crawled across the porcelain. The faded red mouth opened and a voice like dry leaves croaked out.

'And it's time to wake up.'

The bathroom door flew open, the fragile lock snapping like a twig. Caddie and Raggy Maggie vanished like mist before my eyes, and when I turned to the door another familiar face stood there.

'Ameena?'

'The one and only.'

'You… You came back?'

My dad leaned round the door frame. 'We both did,'

he smirked, then he reached into the bathroom and pulled me out on to the landing. Another shock of pain travelled the length of my spine as he tossed me against the wall.

'Get away from me,' I bellowed, shoving him with all my strength. He laughed off the push, then forced me against the wall for a second time.

'Still got some fight in you,' he said, his face right up in mine. 'That's what I like to see.'

I tried to swing at him again, but he leaned back and the palm of his hand cracked against the side of my face, whipping my head to the right. Had he not been holding on to me I would have fallen, but he had me pinned in place with his left hand, as his right hand drew back again.

KER-ACK!

Pain burned like fire across the side of my face, bringing hot tears to my eyes. 'You can stop me, you know?' he said, before another slap exploded across my jaw. 'You can stop me doing this with just a thought. That's what makes you so special, son. That's what makes you unique.'

I brought my hands up over my head to stop him hitting me again. He cackled, then let me slide to the floor. He crouched down next to me. I flinched and pulled back, but the wall stopped me going anywhere.

'You're one of a kind, kiddo. You know that, right? One parent who's imaginary, another who's a real live human being.' He chuckled. 'Well, not exactly *live* any more, but you know what I mean. You're the best of both. You have the ability to imagine *anything in the world*, and the power to make it all come true. You could have been a god.'

He stood up and peered down at me. His nostrils flared in disgust. 'But look at you. Some god.'

The corner of my mouth was sticky with blood. I dabbed it away and glared up at my dad. 'I h-hate you,' I told him.

'I know. I've gone to a lot of effort to make sure of that,' he said darkly. 'The question is, what are you going to do about it?' He held his arms out wide and looked up at the ceiling. 'You want me? I'm right here. Now's your chance to get me back for all those things I've done. Make me suffer. Make me pay. Use that special gift of yours one last time. Take your revenge, kiddo.'

The sparks whirled like a tornado inside me. I stood, feeling taller and stronger than I'd ever felt in my life. Ameena took a wary step backwards, taking cover behind my dad.

'What are you waiting for?' he demanded, raising his voice. 'Do it. Show me what you've got.'

I shook my head. 'No.'

He kept his arms raised, but lowered his head to look at me. '*No?*' he spat. 'What do you mean *no?*'

'I'm not going to do what you want. I'm not going to let you manipulate me any more.'

His arms dropped. 'Is that a fact?'

'It is,' I said. 'I don't care what you do to me. I won't do what you want. Even if you end up killing me.'

He raised his eyebrows. 'Now then,' he nodded. 'Killing you. That is an idea.'

His hands caught me by the hair and yanked me towards the stairs. I hissed in pain and twisted in his grip, but then the top step fell away and the wallpaper began to whizz past me. My chin hit the banister. My chest hit the carpet. My legs flipped over me and I rolled and tumbled and thudded all the way down to the bottom step.

He was on me before I could get up, dragging me into the hallway, shouting so loudly I couldn't make out a word of it. I caught a glimpse of Ameena peeking round the corner at the bottom of the stairs, and then he was in my face again, his fist like an iron bar across my cheek.

The world whirled wildly, and all colour drained out of it. My mouth moved and something that may have been words came out, but even I couldn't understand what they said.

I fell to the floor and rolled, with no real idea where I was rolling to. There was a *creak* as the door of the cupboard under the stairs was pulled open.

'Aha. Now this should do the trick,' I heard my dad say. I managed to turn and look up just as he stepped out of the cupboard. He was holding a cricket bat, both hands gripping the handle. The bat looked battered and well used. I had a feeling it was about to become even more so.

'N-no,' I croaked, holding an arm up.

'You might not believe it, but this'll hurt me more than it hurts you, son,' he said, bringing the bat up to shoulder height. 'I don't want to do this. I want you to stop me. I'm counting on you stopping me.' He stared at me expectantly. 'I will smash you up,' he warned, and flecks of foam formed at the corners of his mouth. 'I will break you in half and grind your bones to make my bread.'

Veins stood out across his forehead. His eyes were bloodshot and bulging. They watched me as I shakily got to my feet.

'OK,' I said.

He frowned. 'OK?'

'Kill me.'

He laughed at that, my dad. He actually laughed. Then he stopped as suddenly as he had started.

'What?'

'Do it. Kill me. You'll be doing me a favour.'

He seemed to consider this, then he shrugged. 'Fair enough.'

The sparks flickered all through me. They danced behind my eyes, lighting up the world, begging – *demanding* – I put them to use. I saw the bat draw back again, as if in slow motion. I saw the look of demented glee on my dad's face as his grip shifted and he took aim at my head.

And then I saw Ameena. She caught him by the shoulder, stopping him before he could swing. I realised for the first time she was wearing the brown robe, but with the hood down.

'Wait,' she said. 'You'll kill him.'

My dad looked from her to me. 'And?'

Ameena glanced at me. Was that pity I saw in her eyes? Sadness? Regret? 'He's no use to us dead,' she said gruffly.

Probably none of those things then.

'The plan,' she reminded him. 'The plan to save everyone. To bring them through here.'

'Ameena, Ameena, Ameena. There are many plans,'

my dad said. 'Plan A, yes, in an ideal world, would involve us breaking down the barrier and turning this world into the Darkest Corners, thereby saving the poor unfortunate souls trapped over there.' He scowled at me. 'But my darling son is proving to be more stubborn than I thought, so we may have to move on to Plan B.'

'What's Plan B?' Ameena asked.

'I beat him to death with this cricket bat.' He looked at her coldly. 'Do you have a problem with that?'

She hesitated, just for a moment, then shook her head. 'No.'

'Good. Because Plan C involved torturing you while he watched. I bet he still cares about you enough to want to stop that happening.'

He laughed at the look of shock on Ameena's face. 'Just kidding,' he said with a wink. 'You see the thing is, between you, me and my boy here, I've never really cared about saving anyone.'

'What?' Ameena frowned. 'But... but you said...'

'I know what I said. But it was all just an excuse, really.

I wanted free. *Me*. And not just for a few minutes or a few hours like I can do at the moment. Free. Truly free. For ever.

'And I wanted him to suffer, of course,' he continued. 'Suffer like I did, stuck in there, rotting away in the Darkest Corners. I wanted him to feel pain like I had, feel loss like I had.'

He gave a self-satisfied smirk. He was looking straight at me, but talking as if I wasn't even in the room. 'I've killed everyone he loves, and I've made him feel that he's the one to blame. I've stolen his whole life away, just like he did to me. Oh, sure, having him break down the barrier and bring about the end of the world would have been a nice touch. A really fitting finale. But we can't have everything, right? So I'll settle for beating him to death. Maybe he'll man up and try to stop me. Maybe he won't. Either way, I'm chalking it up as a win.'

He raised the bat again.

'I get all that. It's just... after all the planning,' Ameena said. 'When you're so close to getting everything you dreamed of. It just seems like, I dunno, you're giving up. Admitting you can't break him.'

A twitch of anger flitted across my dad's face. For a moment I thought he really was going to turn the bat on Ameena, but he simply glared at her until she stepped aside.

He grinned at me and shifted his grip on the bat's handle. 'This will not be a pretty death,' he said. 'It won't be heroic. It won't be noble. It'll be all broken bones and missing teeth and you giving it "Stop, no, please, stop!".' His eyes blazed. 'But I won't. I'll never stop. I want you to be very clear on that.'

I swallowed. I straightened my back and held my head high and thought of my mum.

'Get a move on,' I said. 'I haven't got all day.'

He roared. His muscles tightened.

And he swung.

Chapter Six

READY AT LAST

The bat *whummed* by just centimetres above my head. I exhaled.

My dad was staring at me. He was still holding on to the bat with both hands, but it pointed down towards the floor now.

From the corner of my eye I could make out shapes in the darkness, half-formed apparitions lurking in the gloom. The things from the Darkest Corners were gathering, watching and waiting, preparing for the moment when the wall would come tumbling down.

I inhaled.

Ameena had her back against the wall, not looking at me. She was focusing on my dad and the weapon in his hands.

I exhaled.

'He didn't flinch,' my dad said, and it sounded as if he was talking to himself. 'He didn't even flinch.'

The sparks crawled like ants inside me now, no longer rushing, no longer zipping furiously around. They had finally accepted – *I* had finally accepted – that I was not going to put them to use.

He had gone too far, pushed too hard. Everything, every part of me, was numb. It no longer mattered what my dad did to me, or what any of them did to me. I was done. I was spent. I had seen all the horrors the world had to offer, and I was too sick and tired to see any more.

'You're bolder than I gave you credit for, kiddo,' he said. He smiled, flashing his teeth. 'Of course, you get that off your dad.'

'But you're not my dad.' He opened his mouth to argue, but I jumped in first. 'My father, maybe. But not my dad. Never my dad.'

Silence filled the hall. They were both watching me,

waiting to see what I'd do next, but I just stood there and told it like it was.

'I can see them, you know? Over there in the Darkest Corners. I can feel them too, waiting for the wall to come down. Waiting to come through here and run riot over this world. I can hear them, and I hope they can hear me too. If they can, I want them to listen because I want them to know something.' I turned my head to the ghostly shapes and raised my voice. 'I want them to know that this is as close as they're ever going to get.'

I raised my gaze to my dad. His face was in shadow, but I could see the rage building behind his eyes. 'You can't do anything more to me,' I told him. 'You can try – I'm sure you'll try – but there's nothing you can do that's worse than what you've already done. There's nothing left you can take away from me.' I allowed myself a grim smile. Despite everything, it was a smile of victory.

'You've lost,' I told him. 'Even if you kill me, you've lost.'

I braced myself for an explosion of anger that never

came. Instead, my dad slowly turned his head to Ameena and nodded. When he turned back to me his face had changed. Softened somehow.

'In that case,' he told me, 'I think you're ready.'

That caught me off-guard. 'Ready?' I asked. 'Ready for what?'

His head twitched in the direction of the living room. 'Doctor?'

'Doctor?' I gasped. 'Doc Mortis?'

He nodded. 'The one and only.'

And in he came, strolling through from the living room like it was the most ordinary thing in the world. Doc Mortis looked like he had always done – short and squat, with wispy white hair and a bloodstained white coat.

But he wasn't exactly the same. There was a red mark round his throat, like a burn, and his face was crisscrossed with fiery scratches. He had survived the attack by one of his own patients, but he hadn't survived unscathed.

He looked over at me, and I saw that a wide strip of his scalp had been ripped away, leaving a mess of half-congealed blood behind. His glasses were bent out of shape, both lenses cracked beyond any use whatsoever. But still he kept them balanced on the edge of his nose. He peered over them at my dad.

'You called?' said Doc Mortis, drawing the words out in that creepy Eastern European accent of his.

'He's ready.'

'Are you sure?'

'I'm sure.' My dad stepped back and gestured at me. 'It's time. Wake him up.'

There was a *snap* as Doc pulled on a pair of thin rubber gloves. From nowhere he produced a syringe with a long slender needle fixed to the end.

'What are you doing?' I asked. 'What is he doing?'

'Relax, Kyle,' said my dad, and I suddenly couldn't remember him ever having used my name before. He caught me by the arm and held me in place. 'It'll all be over soon.'

There was a sensation like a wasp sting at the side of my neck as Doc stabbed in the needle. My dad smiled, and there was something like concern there in his eyes. That was another first. 'We're bringing you back to us,' he said. 'We're bringing you home.'

And at that, the last of the blue sparks faded, and a calming darkness fell in their place. The pain that stabbed through my limbs became soft and fluffy like candyfloss. It tickled across my skin before being carried off on the wind. I felt my heart flutter like a rabble of butterflies and a tingling spread out from where the needle had pierced my skin.

And then nothing but darkness.

And then no one but me.

And then...

And then...

A sound somewhere in the nothing. Far away. A sound I recognised. A sound I knew.

BEEP.

BEEP.

BEEP.

The sound of a heart monitor.

The sound of a hospital.

BEEP.

BEEP.

BEEP.

And in the darkness, a giggle. A child's voice, soft and high-pitched.

'Oh, look, Raggy Maggie. Mr Lazy Bones is finally waking up.'

Chapter Seven

MR LAZY BONES WAKES UP

Light. It brightened the space beyond my closed eyelids, easing me awake. I lay still, unable to move, and immediately thought of my first encounter with Doc Mortis. He'd drugged me and strapped me to an operating table. I hadn't been able to move then, either – only been able to watch silently as he'd drawn closer with his bag of rusty tools.

But I *could* move now, I realised. As my body began to wake up, my hands twitched and my arms raised to pull against the straps holding me down.

Only there were no straps holding me down. Not on my arms, not on my legs, not across my forehead like last time.

I opened my eyes. The room I was in was stark and bare, but it was clean. There was no flaking paintwork or bloody streaks on the wall. In fact, there wasn't much of anything. The walls and the ceiling were white. There was no furniture, aside from the bed I was lying on. The place looked less like a room than a template for a room, like something that would eventually become a room when the owner decided what he or she wanted to put in it.

I tried to sit up and regretted it immediately. The room spun and a sharp pain hacked at my skull. There was a thin white sheet covering my body. I threw it off and saw that my legs were bare. From the knees up I was covered with a hospital gown, which I could feel was open at the back. Despite the situation, I was relieved to note that I was still wearing underwear. If I was going to have to run away from something, I didn't fancy doing it with no pants on.

I lay back on the pillow and the pain in my head subsided to a level I could cope with. There were wires attached with sticky pads to my chest, but the other end of each wire hung loosely over the sides of the bed. It was a hospital bed, with raised metal guards at either side to stop me rolling out. A proper *modern* hospital bed, not the rusted old contraptions in Doc Mortis's hospital.

There was a *click* as a door was opened somewhere behind me. I twisted my head round and saw two men stepping into the room behind me. It was my dad and Doc Mortis. They approached in a rush, side by side, until they reached my bedside.

'Where am I? What have you done to me?' I demanded.

'Relax, Kyle,' my dad said. He was wearing a long white coat with a badge fixed to the left-hand breast pocket. The badge displayed the little logo of the National Health Service and a name: Dr Feder. 'You will be very disorientated. You've been through a traumatic experience.'

He shone a small torch in my eyes, but I batted it quickly away.

'Oh, you think?' I snapped. 'And whose fault is that?'

He raised his eyebrows towards Doc Mortis, who made a hasty scribble on a clipboard he carried. Now that I looked at him, there was something very different about

Doc. He was the same short, squat shape, but his scars were gone and his broken round glasses had been replaced by black-framed rectangular ones. His hair was still thin and wispy, but the strip of exposed flesh across his scalp had disappeared.

His clothes were different too. Or rather, his clothes were the same, but they were now clean. His white coat was exactly that – white, without a single bloodstain to be seen. He had an NHS badge pinned to his chest too. It read: Dr Morris.

'Kyle,' said my dad, and his voice was more gentle than I'd ever heard it. 'Do you know where you are?'

'Not really,' I admitted. 'The Darkest Corners? Although probably not. I'm no use to you over there, am I?'

Both men shared a confused look. Doc quickly wrote something else on his clipboard.

'You are in hospital,' my dad said. 'Do you remember why?'

'Because you threw me down the stairs and he stabbed a needle in my neck,' I retorted. 'At a guess.'

There was that look of confusion again, with a dose of concern mixed in. 'You were assaulted,' he continued. 'On Christmas Day. Do you remember?'

'Of course I remember! Mr Mumbles. How could I forget that?'

Doc's pen scratched furiously against his paper. My dad looked down at the notes and gave a faint nod.

'I'm afraid I don't know what that means,' he told me. 'I don't know who Mr Mumbles is.'

'Yes, you do,' I growled. 'You sent him.'

'You were alone in your house,' my dad continued, a little flustered. 'And became aware of an intruder trying to gain entry. He tried to come through your bedroom window at first. Then he tried to come in through the doors.'

He spoke slowly and deliberately, pausing at the end of each sentence to give me an encouraging nod.

'Finally he gained entry through the window in your living room. You tried to escape, but he caught you.'

'I know all this,' I said. 'Why are you telling me? What are you doing? What's all this about?'

'He caught you and... he hurt you, didn't he? He was strong, and he was violent, and he wasn't holding back. He beat you badly. He was the one who threw you down the stairs.'

'No! It was you!'

'That's not true, Kyle. I would never hurt you. I'm your d—'

'You're not my dad!' I cried. 'Stop saying you're my dad!'

He stopped, and I could see from his face that he was taken aback. He cleared his throat. 'Doctor,' he said. 'I'm your doctor.'

Something tingled at the base of my skull. It nestled back there, an itch I couldn't quite scratch.

'What?' I said. 'What are you talking about? What are you trying to do?'

'You received a severe head trauma, Kyle,' he continued. 'There was serious bleeding in your brain and we believed there was a very good chance you were going to die. We had no choice but to operate. Afterwards we induced coma, in order to allow the brain to recover.'

The word came out of me all by itself. 'Coma? What... what do you mean "coma"?'

'You have been asleep for almost a month, Kyle.'

'What...? No, I haven't. No. I've... I've...'

'You were lucky. We almost lost you several times.' He finally smiled. It was a smile of relief. 'But you pulled through. You're a real fighter.'

'Pulled... pulled through?' I mumbled.

'Your mother is waiting outside,' said Doc Mortis. It was the first time he'd spoken since entering the room, and I noticed immediately that his accent was gone. 'Would you like to see her?'

'My... my mum?' I said. The inside of my head was reeling like a roulette wheel. 'My mum's dead.'

Again that pen, scribbling on the clipboard. My dad – my doctor? – patted me on the arm. I flinched and drew back, but he didn't seem to notice. 'You've been dreaming, Kyle,' he said. 'It's very common. Your mum's fine.' He nodded to Doc Mortis, who smiled at me, then scuttled off towards the door.

My dad turned back to me. 'He'll go fetch your mum.'

'What is all this?' I demanded. 'This isn't a hospital.'

'What makes you say that?'

I tugged on the wires sticking to my chest. 'Well, these aren't attached to anything for starters.'

A puzzled frown furrowed his brow. 'Yes, they are,' he said. 'They're all attached to these.' He gestured to an empty space beside the bed. 'Monitoring equipment mostly, for keeping track of how you're doing.'

'Are you mental?' I scowled. 'There's nothing there.'

He stared at me, and there was that expression of concern again. 'Yes, Kyle. There is. Look. It's all right here.'

And suddenly he was right. I could see them there – three little screens all blinking and flashing their reams and reams of data. Two were built into a tall narrow trolley; the other was attached to a metal pole. A clear bag hung at the top of the pole. Liquid dripped along a tube that I now realised was inserted into the back of my hand.

I made a grab for the tape that held the tube in place,

but my dad put a gentle hand against my head and held it there until I stopped struggling.

'Relax,' he said. 'Like I say, you've been through a lot. All these reactions are understandable. All this must come as a shock.'

I watched the liquid trickling down the tube. 'Trust me,' I croaked. 'You have no idea.'

The door opened and Doc Mortis poked his head round the frame. He raised his eyebrows expectantly.

'One moment,' said my dad. He turned back to me. 'Your mum is waiting to see you,' he said. 'But before I bring her in, I need to be confident you're OK. You can... You can see the equipment now, right?'

I looked over to the screens that hadn't been there a few moments ago, and gave a slow nod of my head. 'Yes.'

'And what about the rest of the room? What can you see, Kyle?'

The rest of the room was empty. Same blank walls. Same stark ceiling. 'Nothing,' I told him. 'There's nothing here.'

His hand squeezed my arm. 'Try,' he encouraged. He motioned up towards the corner of the room. 'What about the television? Can you see the TV?'

I followed his gaze. 'No.'

'It's there, Kyle,' he said. 'It's important that you see it before we bring your mother in. It's important I know you're OK.' He pointed to the corner up by the ceiling again. 'The TV. Do you see it?'

'No. I... I...'

'It's a flatscreen, twenty-eight inch, black frame with silver writing at the bottom,' he pressed. 'Try to see it. You must try.'

A tingle buzzed at the base of my brain.

'I... I can't,' I began.

'Flatscreen. Twenty-eight inch. Black frame with silver writing at the bottom,' he insisted. 'Concentrate.'

'It's not... There's not...'

But now there was something there. It appeared between blinks of my eyelids: not there one moment, fixed to the wall the next. A flatscreen TV, twenty-eight inch, with a black frame and silver writing at the bottom.

'I see it,' I said, and a sensation of relief washed over me.

'What else?' asked Dr Feder. 'What else do you see?'

From the corners of my eyes I saw the rest of the room appear, as if being painted into place by some invisible brush. There was a sink in the corner, a bottle of bright orange liquid soap mounted on the wall just above the silver taps.

Over there, beneath the TV, was a chair with wooden arms and a tired-looking fabric back. There was a window beside it. The blinds were closed, but a dozen or more "Get Well Soon" cards sat on the sill. A dozen or more! I couldn't think of a dozen people who'd want to send me a card, but there they were all lined up in a row.

'Everything,' I said. 'I see everything.'

He looked around the room, as if seeing it through my eyes. Then he rocked back on his heels and gave a satisfied nod. 'Excellent. You've done really well, Kyle. Would you like to see your mum now?'

My head gave a slight jerk up and down and my eyes

went to the door. Doc Mortis, or whoever he was, looked happy as he pushed the door fully open and stepped aside.

And there she was. My mum. Standing in the doorway, her eyes glistening with tears, her whole body trembling. She ran at me and her arms and her smell were suddenly around me. Her hair tickled my face, and my dad and Doc Mortis no longer mattered. Nothing mattered except her, and that moment, and that hug.

'You're OK,' she sobbed when she finally pulled away, and they were tears of happiness and relief. Just like mine.

'So are you,' I said, sniffing loudly. 'You were... I mean, I thought you were...'

She hugged me again, and all my doubts drained away in her arms. It was her. She was real. She was mum.

When we pulled apart I looked over at Dr Feder. 'I thought... My dream. You were my dad.'

My mum gave an embarrassed laugh and her cheeks tinged pink. She glanced at the doctor, with his broad shoulders and square jaw, then quickly looked away.

'You woke up a few times before we operated,' he

explained. 'You would've seen me then. Doctor Morris too. That would explain how we got into your dreams.'

There was that itch again. That niggle at the back of my head.

'Yeah,' I said. 'I suppose it would.'

'Anyway, I'll leave you to it,' Dr Feder smiled. He strolled over to the door and made his way out into the corridor. Just before he left, he turned back to me. 'You had me worried there for a while, but you came through.' His smile widened. 'I knew you could do it, kiddo,' he said, and then he closed the door with a *click*.

Chapter Eight

THE TRUTH IS OUT THERE

It was an hour or more before my mum moved away from the side of the bed. She sat there, perched, listening to me tell her all about Mr Mumbles and Caddie and Ameena and all the others.

'I knew we shouldn't have talked about that Mr Mumbles,' she said, stroking my forehead. 'Trust your nan, filling your head full of nonsense.'

I frowned. Of course. The conversation about my old imaginary friend over Christmas dinner had happened. *Really* happened, I mean. It was later that the *intruder* came. I tried to remember back to that moment, but the only image that came to mind was of Mr Mumbles in his hat and coat with his mouth sewn tightly shut.

'Nan,' I said, pushing the thought away. 'Is she all right?'

Mum smiled. I had looked closely for any sign of stitching round her face, any sign that she wasn't who she said she was, but I had found nothing.

'She's fine. Worried about you. But she's fine.' Mum stole a look towards the door. 'I should phone her. Let her know.' Her hand reached for mine and squeezed it. 'But not quite yet, eh?'

'Did they catch him?' I asked. 'The man who... The man?'

Mum shook her head. 'No,' she said. 'Not yet. But they will. Someone saw him attacking you and chased him off.'

'Ameena?'

She looked at me strangely. 'No, Kyle. There is no Ameena, remember? It was a boy from your school. What's his name? Billy.'

I sat up sharply. 'Billy,' I gasped, remembering him in the tower, and then not in the tower as the porter dragged him away. 'I have to help him. They've got him.'

My mum rested a hand on me. It was soft and warm,

and the panic began to ease at once. 'Billy's fine,' she assured me. 'He came in the other day to see you. Brought a card too, I think.'

She got up and looked through the cards. 'Here we are,' she said, passing me one of them. 'It's not in the best taste,' she said, pursing her lips, 'but he assured me it was a joke.'

I looked down at the card. It was a sombre-looking thing with "My Deepest Sympathies" printed across the top. Below that was a picture of a snow-covered church, not unlike the one he'd been taken from.

Hadn't been taken from. *Hadn't.*

It was a sympathy card for relatives of people who had died. Billy's sense of humour was no better in real life than it was in my dreams, apparently.

Inside, in messy handwriting, was a short message. *I totally saved your ass. You're doing my homework for the rest of your life. Get well soon, dweeb*, and then Billy's scrawled signature at the bottom.

'That was nice of him,' I said, handing the card back.

'Hmm,' Mum said, unconvinced. 'But as you can see, nothing bad's happened to him.'

'Yeah,' I said. Then I added, 'Shame, that,' and we both laughed.

I wanted to freeze-frame the moment. Me and Mum sitting there laughing, like everything was right with the world. All too soon, though, it came to an end.

'Right, I better go phone your nan and let her know the good news.' She bent over me and kissed my forehead. 'I won't be long. You want anything?'

'No,' I said, and I really and truly didn't. I didn't want anything, didn't need anything. It was over. The nightmare was over.

Mum kissed me again, said a garbled goodbye, then left through the same door the doctors had, promising to be back in no time at all.

The door closed and I was left alone. I could hear the hustle and bustle out in the corridor, the normal sounds of a hospital at work. *Normal.* That was a word I didn't think would ever enter my head again.

I relaxed into the pillow. The top end of the bed was raised at a slight angle, and as my head sank down, I couldn't remember ever feeling so comfortable. The pain in my head was little more than a niggle.

My eyes closed. I lay still, enjoying the feeling of serenity that had begun to fill me. I didn't have to run any more, hide any more, fight any more. I didn't have to be scared, or be strong, or be anything but a kid.

And then the door opened and spoiled everything.

'That was quick,' I said, opening my eyes, but it wasn't my mum stepping into the room. It was a girl dressed in black, with skin the colour of milky chocolate and boots that looked custom-built for kicking.

She looked around the room before fixing her gaze on me. 'Hey, kiddo,' said Ameena. 'You miss me?'

My body went tense, bringing the pain back to my head.

'You just going to lie there with your mouth hanging open?' Ameena asked. 'Or are you going to say something?'

I just lay there with my mouth hanging open. Ameena

closed the door behind her, then came to the side of my bed. 'You might want to pull yourself together there,' she told me. 'We might not have much time.'

'You're not real.'

'No, I'm not. Well, not in the conventional sense,' she admitted. She gestured at the room around her. 'But then neither is this.'

'I dreamed you,' I said. 'I dreamed you. You shouldn't be here.'

'You're right, I shouldn't,' she said. 'If he finds out I've snuck in to see you, he'll kill me.'

'Who? Who'll kill you?'

'Guess,' she said. Then added, 'Your dad,' before I had the chance. 'The handsome and dashing Doctor Feder.' She put her hand to the side of her mouth and spoke in a mock-whisper. 'Who isn't really a doctor, by the way.'

I could feel my heart racing. The lines on one of the monitor screens peaked like a mountain range and a red light began to blink on and off.

'You're not real,' I said again. 'I dreamed you.'

'No, listen to me,' she said, her voice low, her face serious. 'The other stuff, the imaginary friends, the Darkest Corners. That stuff's real. All of it. This. This here now. This is the dream. This is what isn't real.'

'You're lying,' I said, and the red light on the heart monitor blinked faster. 'This is a trick, or a... I don't know... a hallucination or something.'

I rolled away from her and tumbled out of bed. The wires attached to my chest tore free and all three machines began to shriek in complaint. Ameena flicked the power switch at the wall, silencing them.

'Calm down, kiddo, or you'll get us *both* killed.'

I moved round the bed and shoved past Ameena on my way to the door.

'Get away,' I spat. 'You're not real. None of that stuff was real. I want my mum. I'm going to get my mum.'

'Your mum's dead.'

I stopped at the door. 'Your mum's dead,' Ameena said again. 'Your dad killed her.'

'She's not dead,' I growled. 'I saw her.'

'You think you saw her. He convinced you into seeing her, like he convinced you into seeing all of this.'

'No!' I cried, and I pushed through the door and out into the corridor. I stopped when I got there. I could still hear the hospital sounds bustling around me, but the corridor itself was empty.

And I mean *empty*. The floor was bare wood, the walls a glossy white. The *corridor* was nothing more than a short, narrow hallway with a door at each end and an opening that led on to an equally featureless stairway.

All those old feelings of panic and dread began to bubble furiously in my gut. I carried on towards the opposite door just as Ameena came through the one behind me.

The door opened on to a hospital day room. There were a few tatty armchairs and a mismatched couch in one half of the room, with a boxy old TV set squashed into the corner.

Three men and one woman sat on the chairs, reading magazines, doing crosswords, or just dozing gently in their dressing gowns. None of them looked up as I stumbled in.

The other half of the room was as blank as the hallway outside. There was a single window on the otherwise featureless wall, the blinds pulled half closed. I could see a darkening evening sky between the slats, but nothing more.

Some random pieces of medical equipment stood in the bare half of the room. A blood-pressure monitor. Some sort of ECG machine. One of those things they use to shock stopped hearts back into action. A defibrillator, that was it.

'What is this? What's going on?' I demanded. Still no one in the day room looked my way.

'He convinced you that you were in hospital. Your mind started filling in the details,' Ameena said. 'But then it stopped.'

'Details? What do you mean details?'

'This,' she said, gesturing around us. 'The whole thing. The whole hospital. It's not real.' She frowned. 'Well, no, that's not true. It *is* real now. But it wasn't back then.'

'What are you talking about? Back when?'

'Back then. Back before you created it.' She paused a moment to let that sink in.

'Created it?'

'You still don't get it, do you, kiddo?' she said. 'You still don't understand what you're capable of. The stuff Doc Mortis stuck in your neck – that needle – it was designed to make you open to suggestion.'

My hand went to my neck. Was there an ache there? I wasn't sure.

'Your dad doesn't usually need that sort of thing. He can be pretty damned persuasive all on his own. But you were too stubborn, so he had to drug you first.'

'Drug me...? I don't... No, none of this is happening.'

'He convinced you it was all a dream. Convinced you that you were actually safe in hospital, and that none of the rest of it had really happened.' She smiled sadly. 'And, man, I bet you wanted to believe that, kiddo. I bet your mind raced to believe it, to picture it, to imagine it was all true. But your mind isn't like anyone else's. You wanted it to be real and so it became real. The hospital. Your mum. All of it. You created your own little safe haven. Your own happy ending.'

My mouth was dry. 'No,' I croaked. 'No, that's not true.'

'Sorry, kiddo, but it is. Every word of it.' Ameena looked down at the floor, considering her next few words carefully. 'He needed you to use your abilities. He needed one more big push to bring the barrier down and let the Darkest Corners in. He couldn't force you to do it, so he tricked you instead.' She cleared her throat gently. '*We* tricked you instead. We tricked you into opening the door.'

'There is no door,' I said through gritted teeth. 'There is no Darkest Corners.'

She pointed in the direction of the window. 'Take a look.'

I followed her finger, but didn't move. Not at first, anyway. Then, ignoring the pain in my grinding knee, I took a small, tentative step towards the window. Ameena gave me a nod of encouragement when I turned to look at her, and then I was there, standing before the blinds. I took a deep breath. I pulled the string to open the slats all the way. And then I looked, and the blood in my veins turned to ice.

What had I expected to see? I wasn't sure. An empty street. One or two late-night wanderers, maybe.

But not this. Never this.

There were hundreds of them. *Thousands*. They scuttled and scurried through the darkness, swarming over the village like an infection; relentless and unstoppable.

I leaned closer to the window and looked down at the front of the hospital. One of the larger creatures was tearing through the fence, its claws slicing through the wrought-iron bars as if they were cardboard. My breath fogged the glass and the monster vanished behind a cloud of condensation. By the time the pane cleared the *thing* would be inside the hospital. It would be up the stairs in moments. Everyone in here was as good as dead.

The distant thunder of gunfire ricocheted from somewhere

near the village centre. A scream followed – short and sharp, then suddenly silenced. There were no more gunshots after that, just the triumphant roar of something sickening and grotesque.

I heard Ameena take a step closer behind me. I didn't need to look at her reflection in the window to know how terrified she was. The crack in her voice said it all.

'It's the same everywhere,' she whispered.

I nodded, slowly. 'The town as well?'

She hesitated long enough for me to realise what she meant. I turned away from the devastation outside. 'Wait... You really mean *everywhere*, don't you?'

Her only reply was a single nod of the head.

'*Liar!*' I snapped. It couldn't be true. This couldn't be happening.

She stooped and picked up the TV remote from the day-room coffee table. It shook in her hand as she held it out to me.

'See for yourself.'

Hesitantly, I took the remote. 'What channel?'

She glanced at the ceiling, steadying her voice. 'Any of them.'

The old television set gave a faint *clunk* as I switched it on. In a few seconds, an all-too-familiar scene appeared.

Hundreds of the creatures. Cars and buildings ablaze. People screaming. People running. People *dying*.

Hell on Earth.

'That's New York,' she said.

Click. Another channel, but the footage was almost identical.

'London.'

Click.

'I'm... I'm not sure. Somewhere in Japan. Tokyo, maybe?'

It could have been Tokyo, but then again it could have been anywhere. I clicked through half a dozen more channels, but the images were always the same.

'It happened,' I gasped. 'It actually happened.'

I turned back to the window and gazed out. The clouds above the next town were tinged with orange and red. It was already burning. They were destroying everything, just like *he'd* told me they would.

This was it.

The world was ending.

Armageddon.

And it was all my fault.

Chapter Nine

TAKING BLAME

I watched for a few more seconds before the horror of it all became too much. I turned away from the window. Ameena hadn't moved, and nor had any of the people in the chairs. They continued their reading and their puzzle-solving and their dozing like they were off in some different world that wasn't in any way connected to this one. I envied them that.

'I did this,' I muttered as the truth began to sink in. 'Everything out there. The world. People dying. I did this.'

Ameena nodded. 'Yep, you did,' she said. I shot her a wounded look, but she didn't flinch from it. 'The question is, what are you going to do about it?'

'Do? What can I do? I can't stop that. No one can stop that.'

'You've got special abilities that no one else has.'

'Not any more!' I cried. 'Don't you get it? This is the Darkest Corners now. I'm powerless in the Darkest Corners. That's why the hospital isn't finished, because the barrier came down while I was still creating it. Don't you see? It's over. It's too late to stop anything. I'm a kid. I'm just a kid.'

She chewed her lip. 'But you're going to try, right?'

'Try what, Ameena? Try *what*?' I demanded. 'What can I try against all that? And... and why are you even here, anyway? You work for *him*, remember? You're on his side, not mine. You made that very clear. You should be out there celebrating with the rest of them. With your *own kind*.'

That hurt her. Her eyes widened a little and the corners of her mouth tugged down just a fraction. She spoke, and when she did, it was in a voice on the brink of cracking.

'I didn't want this,' she said. 'I didn't want any of this.'

'Yes, you did,' I said, turning my back on her. 'You've been working towards it from the start. How many times did you try to get me to use my powers? How many times did you actually convince me, or trick me, or find some way to force me into doing it?'

I spun back to face her, suddenly furious. 'I'm wrong, what I said; this isn't my fault. It's *your* fault. Yours. If it hadn't been for you none of this would be happening. If it hadn't been for you, everyone would still be alive!'

There was a crash from the stairs, and the grunt of something big and angry. The thing I'd seen outside was on its way up. The monsters were coming to finish me off, but I couldn't summon the energy to care.

Ameena glanced to the door, then back to me. 'Want me to close it?'

I shrugged. Maybe this was for the best. Maybe this was the way it should end. At least then it *would* end, one way or another.

'He tricked me too, you know?' Ameena said. The echo of the creature's grunts bounced further into the day room.

'He told me he wanted to save the good ones. The kids, like me, who were stuck over there with the rest of them. He said he wanted to take us all out of there.'

'And what about when it all started?' I snapped. 'When you saw what he was doing? To me. To Marion. To my mum and everyone else. You still stuck with him. You still helped him!'

Ameena nodded quickly. 'He gets into your head. He can twist the way you think, the way you feel. It's like he can rewire your brain. Mr Mumbles didn't want to kill you. Not at first. Not until your dad persuaded him.'

The sounds of the thing on the stairs were louder than ever, so loud I almost expected it to come leaping through the open door, claws flashing, teeth bared.

'So what?' I asked. 'You're saying he was controlling you?'

'Yes. No. I mean, not really. He just told me everything we were doing was for the best, and he made me believe it.' Her voice cracked and a tear ran down her cheek. 'Every bad thing he did to you, to everyone you cared about, he made me believe it was the right thing to do and... and I'm sorry. I'm so sorry.'

I clenched my jaw. I should hate her. I wanted to hate her. But Mr Mumbles himself had warned me my dad could get into your head and make you do things you didn't want to. He was a manipulator, and maybe I wasn't the only one he'd been manipulating this entire time.

'Close the door.'

Ameena wiped her sleeve across her cheek. She pushed the door closed just as a monstrous shape reached the top of the stairs. There was a loud *BANG* as it hammered against the wood.

'It'll break through,' she warned, jamming her foot and one shoulder against the wood. 'We don't have long.'

'I don't need long.'

I hurried over to the defibrillator and studied the controls. There was a switch marked *ON*. That bit was simple enough. I pressed it and a little green light illuminated inside the button.

There was a dial marked *CURRENT*. Again,

straightforward enough. I cranked it up to full, then carefully removed the shock pads. One was marked *STERNUM*, the other marked *APEX*. The sternum was round the chest area, I knew, but what the apex was I had no idea. Still, I didn't suppose it mattered.

There was a button on the back of one of the pads. The word *CHARGE* was printed on it. I pressed it and the machine began to emit a high-pitched whine.

I wheeled it into position across from the door. Being careful not to touch them together, I gripped both pads and held them by my side. The wires attaching them to the machine were coiled like old-style telephone cables, which meant I'd have plenty of room to manoeuvre.

'OK,' I said. 'Open the door.'

The monster on the other side thumped hard against it. Ameena stared at me in disbelief. 'Open it? Are you nuts?'

I shrugged. 'We'll find out in a minute.' I readied myself. 'Do it. Now. And stay out of sight.'

Ameena yanked open the door just as the brute hurled itself again. It came charging through, its long arms swinging, a serpent-like tongue flicking across its bulging eyeballs.

It ran straight for me, grunting and snorting through its snout of a nose. I dodged as it made its final lunge, brought up both pads and clamped them down on to the monster's head.

There was a sound like a camera flash going off. I felt a jolt travel the length of my arms. The creature's whole body went rigid for a moment, then it clattered against the wall, bounced off and fell to the floor.

We watched it for a few moments, hoping it wouldn't get back up. After a while, I nudged it with my bare foot. It didn't react, and I realised it was quite probably dead.

'I think you're supposed to say "Clear" before you use those things,' Ameena said.

'Oh yeah,' I said, still staring at the fallen monster. '*Clear.*'

I put the pads back into their holders on the side of the defibrillator and switched the machine off. My fingers traced along the button and down the metal case.

'I made this,' I said. The idea seemed alien. Yes, I'd used my abilities to create things before, but nothing this complicated. And I hadn't even been thinking about it. My head spun. Just how powerful had my abilities been? Now I would never know.

'So,' Ameena began. She had her hands in her pockets and was swinging one foot idly above the floor. 'We OK?'

I should hate her. I wanted to hate her.

'No,' I told her. 'We're not.'

'Oh. Right, yeah,' she said. 'I mean... that's fair enough.'

'Why you?'

She raised her eyes to mine. 'What?'

'Why you? Why did he send you?'

Ameena shrugged. 'He brought me up.'

'He what?'

'He brought me up. He's your dad, but you see... Well, he's my dad too.' She smiled weakly. 'I'm your sister, kiddo.'

My mouth dropped open. 'You're my *sister*?' I spluttered. 'But... but... *I kissed you!*'

'Yeah, I know, ya sicko,' she said.

'My *sister*?'

A smile cracked across her face. 'Nah, not really,' she grinned. 'Just kidding.'

I almost smiled. Almost. But a sudden swelling of anger pushed it aside. 'You don't get to do that,' I said, grabbing her by the shoulders. 'You don't get to do that any more! You don't get to make jokes and laugh and pretend like everything's OK. Everything is *not* OK! Everything is never going to be OK again!'

I shoved her harder than I meant to. She gave a yelp as she tumbled to the floor beside the fallen thing. She peered up at me through a curtain of hair and did her best to fight back tears.

'You hate me. I get that,' she said. 'But what you said earlier, about me picking him over you, that's not right. As far as I knew there was only ever him. He's not my dad, but he may as well be. He saved me when I landed in the Darkest Corners.'

She glanced at the monster lying dead on the

floorboards. 'Saved me from things like that. I would've been killed if it wasn't for him. Or worse. He looked after me and fed me and kept me safe.' A tear broke through her defences. She whipped it quickly away. 'And now I see he was using me the whole time. He was preparing me for this. He didn't care about me. He doesn't give a damn about anyone. He just thought I could help him get to you. And it turned out he was right.'

Her voice had been growing weaker with every word. The last few came out as barely a whisper. 'So I didn't choose a side, Kyle. I didn't even know there were sides. I wasn't given that choice to make.'

She looked away and hung her head.

I should hate her. I wanted to hate her.

So why couldn't I hate her?

'Choose.'

She lifted her head and blinked. 'What?'

'Choose,' I said. 'I'm giving you the choice he didn't.'

Ameena sniffed and brushed the hair out of her eyes.

'There's no choice to make. It's you, Kyle. It will always be you.' She tried a smile to go with it, but it didn't amount to much.

I held out a hand and was surprised to find it was as steady as a rock. Her fingers trembled as they slipped into mine and I helped her back to her feet.

'So, we're OK now? Do you, like, you know? Forgive me?'

'No. I can't. I mean, not yet, anyway. I want to believe you. I want to trust you again, like I did. But I can't. Not yet.'

She gave a resigned shrug. 'Maybe someday, huh?'

'Maybe someday.'

Ameena followed me over to the window. The whole village was in chaos, with more fires burning and more grotesque shapes lumbering through the streets.

'There's no snow,' I realised.

'Yeah, don't really know what happened there,' she admitted. 'Don't even know where it came from in the first place. It was nothing to do with us.' She looked at me guiltily. 'I mean, you know? Him. He was as surprised as you were.'

I filed that bit of information away. 'Where is he now?'

'I'm not sure,' she admitted. 'But he's planning on setting himself up in power. He likes the idea of being in charge.'

'In charge? Of that?' I said, motioning at the rampaging creatures below. 'How can anyone take charge of that?'

'Not everyone from over there is a monster,' she said defensively. 'They're the minority. A very vocal minority, I'll give you, but still a minority.'

'What about Billy? Where did they take him?'

'I don't know.'

'Well, think,' I told her. 'You're my person on the inside.'

'I thought I was your trusty sidekick?'

'Well, now you're both. Think. One of Doc's porters took him from the church.'

'Hospital then, probably.' She caught my next sentence before it came out of my mouth. 'Not this one. One that you didn't magic into existence. Could be his own hospital, but probably just the closest one; it wouldn't make any difference to him now.'

'The town then,' I said, looking out at that orange-tinted sky again. The hospital where they'd first taken my mum after she'd been attacked by the Crowmaster was in the next town. It was only a few miles away, but with the streets the way they were, it may as well have been on the moon.

'We've got to try,' I said, speaking the end of that thought out loud. 'We can't just leave him.'

'Well, we could,' Ameena said, then she caught my expression. 'No, of course we can't. What was I thinking?' She chewed her lip. 'Why can't we leave him again?'

'Because he's one of us. He's on our side. He's –' I stumbled over the words – 'my friend.'

'Well, alrighty then,' Ameena said. She gave a slight bow, then gestured towards the door. 'After you.'

I turned and took a few steps towards the door. A familiar figure was creeping cautiously along the hall towards us.

'Kyle?' she gasped. 'What's going on here? Why are you out of bed?'

My legs became heavy and my heart dropped into my stomach. 'Oh,' I whispered. 'Hi, Mum.'

And then I closed the door in her face.

Chapter Ten

SAYING GOODBYE

I stood there with my forehead against the door for several seconds, listening to my mum knocking.

'Kyle? What's going on? Let me in.'

'Is she real?' I asked, not looking at Ameena.

'No. Yes. Kind of. I don't know,' Ameena said. 'She exists. You made her exist. But she's not your mum.'

'She looks like her. She sounds like her.'

'She's your *idea* of your mum,' Ameena said, and I did look at her then. 'She's an impression of your mum as seen through your eyes.'

'What's the difference?'

'Well... everything. She doesn't think like your mum,

she thinks like *you think* your mum would think.' She replayed the words in her head. 'Yeah, that's right.'

Ameena stepped closer to me. Beyond the door, my mum continued to knock and talk.

'Let me in, sweetheart. Open the door and let me in.'

'You know those dolls where you squeeze its hand and it talks or burps or wets itself or whatever?' Ameena said. 'They might look like a real baby. They might pee on your leg like a real baby. But they ain't a real baby. That's sort of what she's like.' She thought for a moment. 'But, you know, without the peeing on the leg stuff.'

'So... she's a doll,' I said. 'She's not real. She's just a talking doll.'

'Yeah. Pretty much,' Ameena said. Then she added, 'Sorry.'

I sucked air in through my teeth. 'Not your fault.'

She shrugged. 'Well, at least that's one thing then.'

I stood back. Then I ran my fingers through my hair, straightened down my hospital gown and pulled open the door. My mum stood there, her hand raised mid-knock.

She shot me an exasperated look and stepped through into the day room.

'What's going on? Why aren't you in bed?' She looked around the room and settled on Ameena. 'And who's this?'

'That's Ameena.'

'Who?' A frown wrinkled her forehead, as if she knew the name, but couldn't quite remember where from.

'Ameena. The girl I told you about.'

'What? No.' She smiled and looked at me as if I were kidding. When she realised I wasn't, her smile died away. 'No, don't be silly. There is no Ameena.'

'There is,' I said, as Ameena waved. 'She's real. Well, more or less.'

'But... she can't be. That was all a dream, that stuff. I mean, how can she be real? She can't be.'

'But she is,' I said softly. 'It was all real. Everything I said.'

'No, but... you said... you said I died.'

'Yes,' I said. My tonsils tightened, making my voice go up an octave. 'I did say that.'

There was silence in the day room then, broken only by the scratching of a pen against a newspaper crossword. Even the sounds of battle outside had quietened, and I felt as if the whole world were listening in on this conversation.

I took her by the arm and led her over to the window. She stared down at the monster on the floor, but didn't comment.

'Look,' I said. 'Look out there.'

She peered through the blinds and I felt her whole body stiffen. I gave her arm a squeeze as silent tears began to roll down her cheeks.

'N-no,' she whispered. 'It can't. It can't be. This... this isn't happening.'

'It is happening. And it's happening because of me,' I told her. 'I did this.'

She stared at me in horror. 'You?'

'Not on purpose. He tricked me. He made me do it. My dad.'

She looked so like my mum. So perfectly, absolutely like my mum. I wanted to tell her this was all just some bad joke and that of course none of it was real. Of course she was still here, still with me, still alive.

But I couldn't. Because she wasn't.

'He killed the person I loved most in the world,' I told her. 'And even though I can't stop all this, I'm going to find him. I'm going to make him pay for what he did.'

Her eyes darted across my face, as if searching for some sign that I wasn't telling the truth. Finally, she stopped searching. Her face paled a few shades. Half a dozen emotions swept like a slideshow across her features. A hand came up and touched my cheek, but there was no warmth to it. No blood flowing beneath the skin.

'I... I feel like your mum,' she whispered. 'I look at you and I see my boy. I see my little boy.'

She lowered her hand. 'But I'm not, am I? I feel like her, but I can also feel it's not right. I can feel *I'm* not right.'

Both hands came up this time. She cupped them round my face and held me. We were both crying now, tears flowing down our faces before falling to the bare wooden floor.

'She loved you, your mum,' she whispered, pulling me in until our foreheads met. 'I know she did because *I* love you, Kyle. So, so much.'

'I love you too, Mum,' I said, but the words just barely made it out. 'I loved her too.'

'She would be so proud of you,' she said. 'So proud of the man you're becoming. My boy – *her* boy – all grown-up.' She clenched her jaw and glanced away.

I threw my arms round her and sobbed against her shoulder. She wasn't my mum, not really. I knew that. But she was the closest thing I'd ever have to my mum again.

'Please,' she whispered. 'You have to go.'

Ameena put her hand on my arm. Reluctantly, I stepped away from this ghost of my mother and saw that the ends of her hair were already becoming hazy and faint.

'There's a man out there who killed your mum. I know what she'd tell you to do if she were here. She'd say not to go after him. She'd say it's dangerous and that she'd never want you putting yourself at risk for her sake. She'd say she wasn't worth it.'

She was right. That's exactly what my mum would have said.

'But we know different, don't we? We know she *was* worth it. Your mum would say not to go, but I'm not your mum, and I say – go get the son of a bitch.'

'You hear the lady, let's go,' said Ameena. I resisted as she began to steer me towards the door, but in my heart I knew I couldn't stay. I couldn't watch my mum – even this version of her – fade away into nothing.

I grabbed one final look at her before Ameena pulled the door closed between us and the day room. Then I strode with renewed determination back to the room I'd woken up in, and tore through the cupboards until I found my clothes.

Twice. He had robbed me of my mum *twice*.

He had hurt or killed or corrupted everyone I had ever really known.

He had turned me into a weapon that was responsible for the Apocalypse that was now taking place all across the world.

And now – now that I finally had nothing left to lose – he was going to pay for it all.

'Whoa! Some warning next time before you go flashing your butt cheeks at me,' Ameena said. She turned away as I slipped my jeans on.

'I wasn't flashing anything. I'm wearing boxer shorts.'

'Whatever. Some warning next time, please.'

I finished pulling on my clothes. They weren't the same ones I'd had on earlier, which was a bit of a relief. I'd been wearing those ones for weeks. The smell of them alone would have warned my dad I was coming.

The clothes I wore now were uniformly dark. Black jeans, black jumper with a black T-shirt beneath. My trainers were also black, but with a silver tick on each side. I tied them in a tight double knot because the last thing I needed was for one to come flying off in the middle of battle.

Battle. The thought made me hesitate. I looked at Ameena, then down at myself. Were we really going to do this? Were we really going to go out there into the chaos and the monsters and who knew what else?

'You scared?' she asked, as if reading my thoughts.

'Terrified. But then I've been terrified since Christmas,' I confessed. I took a deep breath. 'This is the end, isn't it? One way or another.'

'One way or another,' she nodded, then she straightened her shoulders and pulled off a textbook salute. 'It's been an honour serving with you.'

'Whatever,' I said, but inside I smiled. How, after everything, could she still make me smile?

'What's the plan now then?'

'We head to the hospital,' I said. 'We find Billy.'

She looked doubtful. 'Sure that's such a good idea?'

'Yes,' I insisted. 'We don't sell out our friends.'

'Ouch. You're never going to let me forget that, are you?'

'Doubt it,' I admitted, then we headed down the stairs and threw open the door to Hell.

Chapter Eleven

FOUR BY FOUR

Earlier, when the streets had been filled with screechers and beasts, the world had looked like a very scary place. Now it was their turn to flee in terror as things bigger and angrier than they were, ran riot through the village.

Everywhere was dark. The streetlights were out, the few houses that had had lights on were now in darkness, and a thick layer of cloud had covered the night sky. The only glow came from the fires that crackled in buildings and consumed the cars that lay scattered across the roads like discarded toys.

I realised then that it was smoke covering the sky, not cloud. Smoke that was becoming thicker with every home that burned.

We kept low, tucked into the shadows by the door. Grotesque, inhuman shapes moved through the streets, revealed in silhouette whenever they passed the flames. The sounds of screaming and roaring and squealing and growling were all around us. Other sounds too, sounds without description. Sounds I wished I could somehow unhear.

This was the Darkest Corners as I had first seen it, way back on Christmas Day. A place filled with monsters and evil. A place I had mistaken for Hell itself. Or maybe it hadn't been a mistake at all.

'What's the plan? How do we get to the hospital?' Ameena whispered. She'd come from the Darkest Corners too. She'd seen all this stuff before. But her eyes were wide and her hands were shaking with fear.

'We could make a run for it,' I suggested.

'I was kind of hoping not to die, though,' she replied. 'So that rules that plan out. We could try to sneak there.'

'Sneak three miles? That'd take hours. We don't have hours.'

'He could be dead already, you know?' she whispered. 'Just saying.'

'I know. But I have to try. I left him. It's my fault.'

'And you're sure your magic powers are gone?'

I nodded. 'It's the Darkest Corners. I don't have my abilities here.' Just in case, though, I concentrated and tried to bring the sparks rushing through my head. Nothing happened. 'Any other suggestions?'

A thunderous *boom* knocked us back into the doorway. A fireball rose up inside the church, destroying the roof. A cloud of shattered slates and charred wood was lifted into the air with a *whoosh*. As we watched, the pieces began to rain down like missiles, scattering the monsters and leaving the street directly ahead of us clear.

'Running it is then,' Ameena shrugged.

'Police station. There was a car out back earlier,' I said, aiming us in roughly the right direction. The fog made it impossible to see more than a metre or two ahead, which was both good and bad. Good because we couldn't see any of the horrors roaming around, and bad for exactly that same reason.

Shapes moved in the cloud ahead of us, forcing us to change our route. The dust and the smoke were blinding. I had my face buried in the crook of my arm, trying to stop the stuff getting into my lungs. A coughing fit now would be very bad.

The church was still burning, casting an orange glow across the fog. I used it to get my bearings and we hurried on towards the police station.

After a few minutes of running, stopping, dodging and creeping through the fog, Ameena asked the obvious question. 'What if the car's not there?'

'Then we're probably going to die.'

'Right. Just as long as I know.'

The dust was beginning to settle and the smoke was starting to lift. We could see throngs of the creatures through the thinning fog. So far, at least, it appeared they hadn't seen us, but how long that would last was anyone's guess.

We zigzagged down low until we reached the

police station. There were still screechers hanging about on the roof. They were the lucky ones. The broken bodies of others lay scattered around the base of the building. We had no choice but to tiptoe through them as we headed for the car park at the back. The fog was almost completely gone, so we picked up the pace, the need for stealth replaced by an overwhelming urge to move quickly.

Ameena stifled a yelp and I spun round to check on her. A screecher lay on the ground. Or part of it did, anyway. It was a legless torso, with a string of black, poisoned intestines spilling out like spaghetti below its waist. It had both hands on Ameena's leg. The screecher's dark eyes sparkled as it opened its jaws wide.

Her boot crunched against the side of its head. Once. Twice. The screecher lost its grip and we hurried away from it. Out of rage, or frustration, or just plain spite, it let out a scream. The sounds of the darkness changed as everything within earshot turned and looked in our direction.

'Run,' I said, racing for the car park. Ameena was

faster. She pushed me on as dozens of creatures of all shapes and sizes began darting and lumbering and leaping after us.

We turned the corner and I almost cried with happiness. A police 4x4 was parked there, pristine and untouched by the chaos.

Ameena reached it first. She pressed her face against the glass of the driver's door, then let out a whoop of delight. 'Keys!' she cried. 'It's got keys!'

She hauled the door open, then leaned over and opened the passenger door too. I slid awkwardly on to the seat just as the first of the things darted into the car park.

The creature was small but fast. It bounded in frog-like leaps across the car park, closing the gap between us in three long jumps.

Ameena turned the key and the engine spluttered nervously. Then the car gave a throaty roar and lurched forward. Ameena was wrestling with the handbrake when the frog-like thing landed with a soggy *splat* on the bonnet. We both screamed, then she floored the accelerator. The

4x4 lurched forward, stopped, then lurched forward again, tossing me around in the seat.

'What are you doing? Just drive!'

'I'm trying,' she snapped. The entrance to the car park was now swamped with *things*. I was panicking too much to focus on any details. All I could see was the world's ugliest mob, and the near-certain death that awaited us at their hands. Or claws. Or whatever.

Ameena crunched down a gear and tried the pedal again. The car shot forward, the tyres leaving melting rubber on the tarmac. The thing on the windscreen clung on like a limpet as Ameena aimed for the exit.

'Smaller ones, smaller ones, look for the smaller ones.'

'There,' I said, pointing towards something that looked a little like an angry Ewok. Ameena hauled the wheel to the right. The Ewok blinked in the glare of the headlights, and then it vanished beneath the wheels with a meaty *crunch*.

'There!' I pointed again, this time to another of the frog-like things. It burst with a *pop* beneath the front tyres. Ameena shuddered, the wheels slipped, but then we were out of the car park and skidding on to the main road.

My head thumped against the side window and I quickly clipped on my seat belt. 'Can you even drive?' I asked, and my voice betrayed my terror.

'Yeah. That time when Mumbles was after us.'

'That was for, like, fifteen seconds!'

'Yeah, but it was a police car, so I reckon this is more or less the same.'

She dodged round some burning debris, then powered through a group of dog-like creatures, scattering them. The 4x4 rounded another few corners, tore down one monster-infested straight, and then we were out of the village and heading for the town.

We sat there, not speaking, just staring straight ahead through the windscreen. Neither one of us dared to look back. Ameena eventually broke the silence.

'He's quite off-putting, isn't he?'

I nodded. The frog-thing was still clinging to the

windscreen with its sucker-like fingertips. Its bulging eyes flicked back and forth between us.

'Yeah. He is a bit.' I knocked on the glass. 'Oi, mate. Hop it.'

'You sure you can't just magic him away?'

I shook my head. 'I'm powerless now.'

'Yeah, but are you *sure*? This isn't—'

'I can't do it, OK?' I snapped, and that seemed to be the end of it.

'Oh, wait,' Ameena said. She felt around the sides of the steering wheel, then flicked a lever. There was a *clicking* and a light on the dashboard began to flash. 'No, that's indicators,' she muttered.

She moved another lever. The windscreen wipers arced up, taking the frog-thing by surprise. It lifted its hands and leaned back. Ameena slammed on the brakes and the creature rolled off the bonnet. It turned in time to see the 4x4 take off towards it.

It tried to jump out of the car's path, but Ameena threw open her door. It connected with the monster mid-leap, sending it rolling messily across the road. She swerved the car. There was another *pop*, then she pulled back over to the left side of the road and drove on.

'You could've just left it,' I said.

'Had a bad experience with one of those once,' she replied, her eyes fixed on the road ahead. 'Tried to kiss me.'

'Really?'

'Or maybe eat me. It's hard to tell.'

I looked round into the back seat, then down at the dashboard, searching for anything that might be useful. There was a police radio in the car, but it had been switched off. I flicked the switch to turn it on and the 4x4 was filled with screaming and sobbing and the crackle of radio static. A dozen signals all tried to push through at once.

'Help us. Too many of them. Too many to—'

'—happening? What the Hell's happening? Someone—'

'—dead. All dead. Please help me! Something's coming. God, someone help me—'

I turned the radio off again and we continued down the road in silence for a long time.

'We could just keep driving, you know?'

I turned to Ameena. 'What?'

'Just follow the road, see where it takes us. We could make a go of it. Find somewhere we could, I don't know, survive.'

'Survive?' I said. 'With all those things around?'

'People have. People do,' she shrugged. 'I did.'

'You had my dad to look after you,' I said coldly.

'And now I've got you. And you'd have me.'

I stared ahead. 'We go save Billy, then we go find my dad.'

Ameena nodded and we both fell silent again. There was an envelope sitting in a hollow above the glove box. I picked it up and read the name on the front. Then I read it again, just to be sure.

'This is for me,' I said.

Ameena glanced down at the square envelope. 'Open it then.'

The flap wasn't stuck down. I pulled out a handwritten note. '"Enjoy the car,"' I read. '"One final parting gift. Joseph."'

I stuck the note back in the envelope. Even from beyond the grave, Joseph, the mystery man, was still somehow helping me out.

'He must've left it for us. That's why the keys were in it,' I realised.

'That was nice of him.'

I looked long and hard at her. 'Do you know who he was?'

'Not a clue,' she shrugged. 'I know he was starting to get on your dad's nerves a bit, the way he kept interfering, but he didn't have a clue who the guy was. No one did.'

'He was the policeman back at Christmas, remember?'

'Yeah, course I remember.'

'I thought he was an idiot, going on about me pulling his cracker with him, but even then he was helping us. First the message in the cracker itself, then the car parked out back. I bet he planned all of that.'

Ameena drew in a sharp breath and I turned to follow her gaze.

'Whoa.'

The village had been bad, but the town was worse. Fire was spreading through houses and shops. It spread through gardens. It licked across the ground. Even inside the car, we could feel the heat of it on our faces.

Off to my right I could see my school. All the windows were lit up with orange and yellow. I'd dreamed of seeing it burn to the ground since first setting foot in the place, but the sight of it left me hollow. Every last part of my old life was gone.

Ameena slowed the car, but didn't quite stop. Twisted, malformed shapes filled these streets too. They danced around the flames, delighting in the sheer spectacle of it all.

The hospital was on the edge of town, raised up on the hillside. We could only see part of the building, but from here it didn't look like it was burning. Yet.

The 4x4 dipped to one side as Ameena steered it off

the road. 'Direct route,' she explained as the car began to climb the slippery slope.

It was an uncomfortable trip. The hill was grassy and uneven, and the car bounced and rolled its way up towards the low, squat hospital building. We were a hundred or more metres away, but could see the whole place was in darkness.

A thought suddenly occurred to me. 'There'll still be people inside. Won't there? Normal people, I mean.'

Ameena's hands tightened on the wheel. 'Maybe. But if Doc's there...' She didn't finish the sentence. She didn't have to.

I'd seen up close what Doc Mortis could do to people. Even those who were equipped to fight back had felt the sting of his surgical tools. I didn't dare imagine how a hospital full of the sick and injured would fare against him.

'It's a big risk,' Ameena said as the hill began to level off and we approached the rear of the hospital. 'We don't know what's going to be in here.'

'Billy, hopefully,' I said. 'We rescue him, then we can move on to phase two of the plan. Finding my dad.'

She nodded slowly and brought the car to a stop beside the hospital's low boundary wall. 'And what then?'

'Then? Then I'll kill him.'

Ameena's eyes narrowed and her lips went thin.

'You got a problem with that?'

She shook her head. 'No. No problem. If that's what you want.'

'That's what I want,' I said. 'Now kill the lights and let's check the boot.'

'For what?'

'For weapons,' I told her. I looked up at the darkened hospital standing before us. 'If Doc's really in there, we're going to need them.'

Chapter Twelve

THE WRONG DOOR

We'd been hoping for shotguns. We found batons. They were the telescopic kind that extended out to about fifty centimetres and folded down to about twenty. We picked them up and swished them a few times, getting used to the weight.

'He could've left us some hand grenades or something,' Ameena grumbled. 'If he was so keen on helping us.'

'I'm sure he had his reasons,' I shrugged, pulling the boot closed as quietly as I could manage.

'Or a bazooka, maybe.'

I moved towards the wall, keeping low. There was no movement at any of the windows, and I couldn't see anything moving around in the hospital grounds. It was dark, though, and I was all too aware that anything could be hiding in the shadows.

'Door's over there,' Ameena whispered. I followed her finger until I found the main entrance.

'Too obvious. There's another door round the side. We'll go that way.'

'OK. Want me to wait here?'

'No,' I said. 'Why would I?'

'No reason.' She looked up at the hospital and shivered. 'Just hoping.'

'If you don't want to come, you don't have to,' I told her.

'Hey, trusty sidekick, remember?' she said, and she made a passable attempt to grin. 'I've got your back.' Her smile faded and her face became solemn. 'Promise.'

'Right then,' I said. 'Stick close together. Let's go.'

We jumped over the low wall, then discovered it was substantially further to fall on the other side. I landed badly and almost screamed as pain popped in my kneecap. It took a few moments of deep breathing before I could trust myself to open my mouth.

'Forgot about the drop,' I muttered, and we began limping and running towards the main part of the building.

We pressed ourselves against the wall. The windows were a metre above us, too high to see through. But the rooms beyond them were silent and dark.

Keeping my head down, I moved round the building towards the side door. A few moments ago the baton had felt reassuringly solid, but now it slipped in my sweaty hand, and I couldn't imagine it being of any use whatsoever. I gripped it tighter all the same.

'I don't know if these will stop a porter,' I whispered.

'Aim for the legs,' Ameena said. 'They're the weak spots.'

'Oh yeah, I forgot. You're all best friends, aren't you?' I said. It was partly meant as a joke, but it didn't come out that way.

'No. I've never met one, not up close. But anyone living near Doc Mortis learns the best way to deal with a porter.'

She was on the defensive now. 'And it's not like we all just hung about, you know? I grew up terrified of Mortis, hearing all these stories about him. Hearing about what he did to people. I didn't even know him and your dad had some kind of truce figured out until today. I didn't know they were working together. It's not like I was ever kept in the loop.'

I shrugged, but didn't risk replying in case it came out sounding petty or angry. We were nearly at the side door. There was a sensor mounted above it, and it should have slid open at our approach. It didn't move, though, and it occurred to me that the door would probably be locked.

I stopped and studied the toughened glass. The room on the other side was too dark to see into.

'Should we smash it?' I asked.

Ameena elbowed me aside. 'No; stand back. Watch this. You're not the only one with magic powers, you know.'

She clapped her hands once and rubbed them together. Then she pressed her palms flat against the glass. I held my breath and took another step back. Ameena moved her hands to the right, manually sliding the unlocked door out of our way.

She looked back over her shoulder at me and smirked. 'I call that power "common sense".'

'Very funny,' I grunted. I reached above her and held the door open. 'For that, you get to go first.'

'Lucky me,' she said, stepping inside. She glanced in both directions along the corridor, then relaxed. 'There. See? Nothing to worry about.'

A fast-moving shape blurred into her, whisking her away. One second she was there in front of me, the next she wasn't. I dived inside the hospital and heard her muffled screams disappearing along the corridor to my left.

'Ameena!' I called.

Big mistake.

The darkness behind me rustled as something came alive in it. I ran without looking, ignoring my injured knee as I lumbered along the corridor after Ameena, panic acting as the ultimate painkiller.

From up ahead I heard a loud *crack* and the squeal of

something less than human. Ameena gasped as she drew in a breath, then I became aware of her in the dark just ahead of me.

'Watch your feet,' she warned, and I realised the porter was on the floor, thrashing around. 'What did I tell you? Go for the legs.'

We could make out a door in the gloom. She pulled it open and dragged me inside, just as the thing back along the corridor began to pick up speed.

'In here.'

'What is it?' I asked. 'Where does it go?'

'How should I know? Away from them.'

She shoved me forward and I bumped against a shelf. Reaching up, I felt around through the blackness. Yep, there was that horrible sinking feeling again.

'It's a cupboard,' I sighed as she pulled the door closed. 'You've led us into a cupboard.'

I heard her hesitate. 'Well, yeah. I mean *obviously* it's a cupboard.'

We jumped as something began to tap slowly on the

door. *Tap-tap-tap. Tap-tap-tap.* It wasn't fast or hard or frenzied. It was the slow, deliberate knock of something that knew we had no way of escaping. It was in no rush.

Tap-tap-tap, it went. *Tap-tap-tap*, like a cat batting at a mouse it held pinned and helpless beneath its paws. Ameena fumbled around with the handle. There was a reassuring *clunk* as she turned the lock.

'That should keep it out for a while.'

'Great. That'll buy us more time to be stuck in a cupboard.'

'Wait,' Ameena whispered. 'Isn't there always a hatch in the ceiling in these things?'

'That's in a lift,' I said, but she climbed up the shelves and felt around, anyway.

'Nothing,' she groaned.

'See? Told you. Lifts.'

'They really should start to put hatches in the ceilings in cupboards too. We should write to someone.'

'Good idea. Got a pen on you?'

Tap-tap-tap. Tap-tap-tap.

'What are we going to do?' I asked.

'The way I see it, we've got two choices,' Ameena replied. 'We stay here and hope it gets bored and wanders off.'

'Unlikely.'

'Yeah, so that brings us to the second option. We kick the door open and run away.'

Tap-tap-tap.

'I hurt my knee jumping the wall. I can't run very fast.'

'I'm counting on it,' Ameena said. 'If it catches you that'll buy me more time to escape.'

Tap-tap-tap.

'That was a joke, by the way. Too soon?'

'Way too soon.'

Tap-tap-THUNK!

The door shook as something slammed against it from the other side. It hit high above head height, and we both instinctively ducked at the sound.

We listened for more tapping, but there was some sort of commotion going on beyond the door now. Something crunched. A porter squealed. Something went *snap* and the squealing stopped.

It lasted all of five seconds, then we heard nothing more from the corridor.

'What was that?' I whispered.

'Something killing something else,' she said. 'At a guess.'

I reached for the lock and slowly turned it. 'I'm going to take a look.'

Ameena touched me on the arm. 'Be careful.'

'Thanks. I'll bear that in mind.'

The door opened a crack. I almost pulled it closed again as a red glow suddenly flooded the cupboard. A row of emergency lights had illuminated along the ceiling of the corridor. They were only just bright enough to see by, but it was definitely a step in the right direction.

I peered round the side of the door and saw two porters on the floor. The one Ameena had knocked down was where she'd left it, only now it was completely motionless. Its button eyes – one yellow, one black – seemed to point different ways, so it was looking at the ceiling and the floor at the same time.

Another porter lay next to it, its body half leaning against the door. As I pushed, it slumped backwards, its head lolling at an angle that was surely unnatural even for one of them.

'They're dead,' I mumbled, stepping out of the cupboard.

Ameena emerged behind me. 'Right,' she said. 'So they are. Who did that then?'

I looked up and down the corridor. The lights reddened the darkness in both directions, but there was nothing moving either way. 'Not a clue,' I admitted. 'But whoever it was, let's hope they're on our side.'

'Well, at least we know we were right. If the porters are here, Doc won't be far away. The question is, where?'

There was a row of signs on the wall at the end of the corridor. I squinted and read them as we approached. 'That way,' I said, pointing towards the mouth of another corridor that led off the one we were in.

'How come?'

I tapped one of the signs. It read: *OPERATING THEATRE*.

'Ah yes,' Ameena said, and I could hear the shudder in her voice. 'Of course.'

I held the baton ready as we crept along the corridor side by side.

'How long was I out for?' I asked. The question took Ameena by surprise and she only blinked at me in reply. 'After he knocked me out until I woke up in the hospital. Or... you know, whatever it was. How long was I out for?'

'A few hours, I think. Half a day, maybe. Why?'

'Just making conversation,' I whispered.

She nodded. 'Trying to forget about the scary psycho man waiting for us up ahead?'

'Yeah, that too.'

The red lights cast eerie shadows across the walls. Paintings by students from a local art club hung along the walls. A blue-haired clown grinned out from one of them, and I was reminded of Wobblebottom, the clown I'd met in Doc's other hospital in the Darkest Corners. I tried not to think of him as I pushed on through the reddening gloom.

'Two hundred quid for that,' Ameena said. She was looking at a painting of a sheep and shaking her head. 'Who'd want that on their wall? It looks bored rigid.'

'It's a sheep. It's supposed to look bored.'

'Not *that* bored, surely? Poor thing looks suicidal.'

I kept walking and she fell back into step beside me. The corridor was wide, with doors leading off at regular intervals along it. We passed the hospital chapel along the way, and I half thought about popping in for a quick prayer.

But then I heard it from somewhere up ahead. I knew I'd hear it eventually. I'd been waiting to hear it from the moment we stepped through the doors.

'What's that?' Ameena asked. She was straining to hear the music, but I didn't need to. I'd heard it so many times I could recognise it from just a handful of notes.

'That?' I said grimly. 'That's "The Teddy Bears Picnic".'

Ameena clutched her baton in both hands and squeezed it tightly. Even though she hadn't recognised the tune, she clearly understood the significance of it.

'Doc Mortis.'

I began to walk faster along the corridor, heading for the source of the music. 'Doc Mortis,' I confirmed.

And then I ran.

Chapter Thirteen

DANGER DOC

The route to the theatre was clearly marked, but I didn't need the signs to show me the way. I just followed the music instead.

The pain in my knee made my teeth clamp together. I hissed through every step until I finally shouldered through a set of double swing doors marked *ANAESTHETIC ROOM*.

The music shook every surface in there, vibrating the floor and trembling the walls. Ameena came through the doors behind me, but I was already charging for the exit that led into the operating theatre itself.

I clattered against the metal frame of a bed that stood just beyond the doors. The bed was empty, but the white sheets were stained with blood and other fluids I didn't even want to guess at.

There was a second bed squeezed into the small room, and this one was occupied. Billy was strapped to it, his eyes wide and staring, his mouth still sewn shut. He moaned and mumbled as he saw me, and nodded frantically towards the leather cuffs that held him to the bed frame.

'You're alive, thank God,' I said, almost cheering.

Billy was definitely alive, but he looked as if he'd prefer not to be. He was a mess of tears and snot and slick, shiny blood. The blood covered the lower half of his face. It looked even redder in the glow of the emergency lighting.

Ameena sidled in behind me. 'Well, that was easy,' she said. Her eyes scanned the otherwise empty operating theatre. 'Almost too—'

'Don't!' I yelped. 'Don't say it.'

She mimed zipping her lips closed, then shot Billy an apologetic look. 'Oops, sorry. I forgot. You know? About the...' She pointed to her mouth. Billy glared at her. 'I'll shut up now,' she said. She began her lip-zipping mime, then stopped. 'Sorry, doing it again.'

'Don't move, Billy. We're going to get you out of here.'

Billy's eyes went to the straps on his wrists again. Moving wasn't an option for him. I set to work undoing the buckles. The chorus of 'The Teddy Bear's Picnic' continued to chime around us. 'God, I hate that song,' I muttered. 'Find where it's coming from and shut it up.'

Someone tutted from the shadows by the corner. I froze. Even in those *tuts* I could detect the accent. It was Eastern European, but not from any specific country I could identify. It was the sort of accent a bad comedian might put on when making racist jokes about immigrants.

It was the accent of Doc Mortis.

There was a soft *bleep* and the music stopped. 'You are having very poor taste,' he told me. He emerged from the shadows, back to looking like his real self.

It appeared as if a nursery school had used his coat to practise finger-painting on, and that the only colour they had available was red. It was more crimson than white, and it stank of death.

His turkey-like neck had the scar again, and the missing patch of scalp was back. He wore his old glasses too, the round ones with the broken lenses. It was as if the *Dr Morris* version of him I'd seen really was an entirely different person.

I noticed he had a portable CD player clutched in his rubber-gloved hands. He pressed a button on top of the machine and a lid opened smoothly. Doc shook his head, marvelling at the technology.

'The compact discs,' he said. 'Like a record, but smaller. Shinier too. Someone, they took the record and they looked at it and they thought "I can do better than this.".'

I held the baton ready at my side, and saw that Ameena was doing the same. We moved closer together so we both stood between Doc and Billy. But Doc only seemed interested in the CD at the moment. He had removed it from the player and was holding it up, his stubby fingers splayed round the edges.

'Incredible, do you not think? I have never seen one before, until this day. Someone took the record and they improved it. Made it better than it was.' Doc's eyes crept over to me. His rubbery lips parted into a smirk, revealing his yellowing teeth. '*Improved* it, yes? Made it *better*.' He flicked his tongue across the teeth. 'Just like I do.'

'You don't *improve* anyone. You torture them. You mutilate them.'

He waved a dismissive hand. 'You say tomato, I say tomato,' he shrugged, rhyming the first one with *potato*. 'I make art. Is it my fault that no one appreciates my genius?'

'You're not a genius,' I said. 'You're a headcase.'

'The line between the two, it is thinner than you know. Perhaps I walk along the line, yes? Right along its razor edge.'

'Or maybe you're just a sick freak who gets his thrills from hurting innocent people,' Ameena snapped, and there was real venom in her voice.

Doc looked her up and down, starting at the feet and letting his eyes work their way slowly up until they met her gaze. His creepy smile spread across his fish lips again. 'This I will not argue with. But who is innocent these days? You?' He gestured to Billy. 'Him? Anyone? No, no, I do not think so.'

He put the CD back in the machine and pushed the lid closed with one finger. I shifted my grip on the baton. If he pressed *Play* that CD player was getting it. If I never heard 'The Teddy Bear's *bloody* Picnic' again it would be too soon.

Thankfully he didn't start the disc, and the player lived to play another day. He set the machine down on a stainless-steel table and gave me an appraising look.

'Your father, he thinks he is a genius, but he is not. He came to Doc Mortis talking of an alliance. An alliance that would allow me back into the real world. That would allow me a limitless number of new patients for my hospital.'

He brought his left hand up close to his face and I saw he was now holding a surgical scalpel. Doc tilted the knife and the red emergency lights reflected off the polished blade.

'And he did as he said. With my help, of course. He got us back. Here we are. But this means he has outlived his usefulness, I think.' He studied the scalpel. 'I will very much enjoy adding him to my new gallery.'

'Please do,' I urged, and Doc snorted with laughter.

'But you first, real boy. I wished to operate on you in the Darkest Corners, but you escaped. Today, there will be no escape for you.'

'Want to bet on that?' I said, giving the baton a flick. 'We're taking Billy and we're getting out of here. Try to stop us and you'll be the one needing to be hospitalised.'

Doc set down the scalpel. He patted the empty bed with its blood-soaked sheets. A shiver of excitement travelled through him. 'Still warm,' he whispered, then he giggled softly.

I shifted on the balls of my feet and shot Ameena an uneasy look. 'Untie Billy,' I said, then I turned back to Doc. 'I'll watch him.'

Ameena set to work removing Billy's straps. Doc held his hands up in a surrender pose. 'Do not worry. I will not try to stop you,' he said, but a dark glee shone out from his piggy little eyes. He turned his face to the corner opposite him. It too was bathed in shadow. 'He, on the other hand, will do much more than try.'

I realised then that there were not just four of us in the room. There were five. A Frankenstein's monster of a thing took two faltering steps into the light. It was all stitches and scars, a patchwork quilt of skin and sinew sewn together with thick black wire.

It was naked, but a vast, distended stomach protected its modesty. The gut hung down almost to the knees. Things wriggled inside it, pushing outwards, trying to climb right through the flesh.

Ameena undid the last buckle and Billy rolled off the bed. We took cover behind it as Doc's latest patient came waddling closer, its ragged, pieced-together hands grasping for us.

'Do you like?' Doc sniggered. 'This is my all new Patient Zero. One of my finest creations to date. Over here, I have so many exciting tools at my disposal. With this, I have only just scratched the surface.'

The behemoth stumbled and bumped into the bed. Its face was made up of a dozen or more parts. The eyes were different colours. The ears were different sizes. Not even the eyebrows matched.

'A whole ward of the sick and the dying, pieced together to make one perfect specimen,' Doc cackled.

We backed away as the thing began to shamble round the bed. Its stomach heaved and rolled like the surface of the sea. The effect was horrible, but strangely hypnotic at the same time.

It had moved between us and the door, continuing its lumbering route towards us. I was still holding the baton, but I didn't really want to get close enough to use it. The smell of the brute alone was keeping me well back.

'I am very much going to enjoy this,' Doc said. Patient Zero took another step towards us. A melancholy groan escaped through its mismatched lips, and then it stopped advancing.

A hand, each finger a slightly different colour, moved shakily to its chest. One of Patient Zero's eyes widened, while the other narrowed. The hand clutched at where its heart was still presumably located. Then, with a final groan, the monster toppled backwards.

As Patient Zero hit the floor, its stomach burst like a water balloon, but a water balloon filled with rats and bugs and something that looked like custard. I retched at the stink, and jumped back as the insects and rodents squirmed, scampered and squelched in every direction across the floor.

Doc stared down at the definitely dead thing spread out at our feet. The smile fell from his rubbery lips. 'Oh,' he muttered. 'Well, that was disappointing.'

He shrugged and the smirk came back. 'No matter.' Doc interlocked his fingers, then pushed them outwards until the knuckles cracked. 'I will just have to take care of you myself.'

'You?' I snorted. 'Without your porters or your monsters to help you?'

'Kyle, don't,' Ameena hissed, and the fear in her voice made me hesitate.

Doc's grin spread further. 'Ah yes, she knows about me. She has heard the stories of what I can do.'

His arm flicked, little more than a blur. A sharp stinging pain cut across my cheek, and I felt blood run down over my chin. Behind me, embedded into the wall, a scalpel vibrated to a stop.

Doc twitched his arms and two more blades slid down from his sleeves. He caught them in his gloved hands, but Ameena was already bundling Billy and me out of the doors that led to the anaesthetic room. A scalpel stuck deep into the doorframe right beside my head, but then we were through the doors and heading for the next set.

We pulled Billy along, out of the second room and into the corridor. I hobbled as quickly as I could, but I wasn't fast enough. I was holding them back.

'Go! Get away,' I told them, releasing my grip on Billy's arm.

'What?' Ameena spluttered. 'Are you mental? No way am I leaving you.'

'I'll slow you down. Get out to the car and I'll catch up. I'll find you.'

Ameena hesitated, but I shoved them both on. 'I'll come back,' she said.

'Don't you dare. Get to the car. Keep Billy safe. If I don't make it, you're the only one who knows what my dad's done. You're the only one who can make him pay.'

She shuffled awkwardly, then nodded. 'Don't be long,' she said, and then she and Billy were running along the corridor towards the exit.

If you go down to the woods today, you'd better not go alone...

'Great,' I whispered as the music kicked in louder than ever. 'This again.'

The doors to the anaesthetic room swung outwards, revealing Doc silhouetted against the red emergency lighting.

It's lovely down in the woods today, but safer to stay at home...

'Here we are, real boy,' Doc said, shouting to make himself heard. 'It is just you and I now, yes?'

His wrist snapped forward. Metal glinted in the space between us. Instinctively, I raised my arms in front of my face. The scalpel clattered off the baton and fell to the floor.

'A lucky escape,' Doc sniggered. He held up the other knife. 'No matter. For this one, I will get right up close.'

For every bear that ever there was...

He began to run, not the slow, awkward lurching I would've expected, but the sprint of a trained athlete. Caught off-guard, I stumbled back, swinging with the baton as he closed the final few metres.

An arm lashed out and I felt fire across my fingers. A spray of blood hit the wall and the baton joined the scalpel on the floor. I looked at my hand, half expecting to see the fingers gone, but the cut had just sliced through the skin across my knuckles.

The glance to my hand was quick, but by the time I looked back he was right at me, and all I could see were his lips and his teeth and the wiry white hairs that stuck out from each nostril.

Is gathered there for certain because...

My injured knee gave out and I fell beneath him. His own knee jammed against my chest, pinning me to the floor. I drove a fist against the side of his head, sending his glasses spinning across the floor. I hit him again, and this time his face contorted in pain.

Today's the day the teddy bears have—

The music stopped with a *bleep*. Annoyance replaced the pain on Doc's face and he looked over his shoulder in the direction of the operating theatre. 'Huh,' he muttered, then a rubber-gloved hand came down hard on my throat and a scalpel flashed before my eyes.

'Now then, my darling real boy,' Doc whispered, and his voice came out in a cloud of white fog. 'No more with the wasting time. I think it best we operate right here and now!'

Chapter Fourteen

A COLD AND LONELY DEATH

I squirmed beneath him, kicking and twisting as I struggled to get free. His full weight was on me, though, and there was nothing I could do to shake him off.

'What will I do to you, I wonder?' he giggled, and more misty vapour rolled from his mouth. The floor beneath me felt cold. It chilled up through my clothes and numbed my skin.

Doc turned the scalpel over and brought the point closer to my face. I stopped squirming then and tried my best to stay still. The point of the blade was too close for me to see. It was a greyish blur just millimetres from my right eye. Doc's other hand was still on my throat. Even through the glove his touch was cold.

'Shall I take your n-n-nose first?' he whispered, and as

he spoke he started to shiver. He pulled back a little and I saw swirls of cold air rising up from his skin. 'What?' he muttered. 'What is happ—?'

He stopped moving, his face fixed in a frown. A layer of frosty white crept up from inside his bloodstained shirt. It spread like a rash across his scarred throat and carried on right up to the wound in his scalp.

A boy of around five years old leaned round the frozen Doc and showed me his proudest grin. His silvery-grey eyes sparked with mischief.

'I.C.?' I wheezed. It was the boy I'd met in the Darkest Corners. The one I'd saved from Doc Mortis. He'd had the power to freeze things with his touch, but he'd been unable to control it. Apparently in the weeks since then he'd learned how.

'That's my name; don't wear it out,' he said. 'Do it, Big Nose.'

There was a growl and a huge fist connected with Doc's head. He shattered like glass, and a man in a long coat and a wide-brimmed hat was revealed behind him.

'For the last time,' said the man in a voice like gravel, *'don't* call me Big Nose.'

'It's not my fault you've got a big nose,' I.C. said. 'You're so touchy about it. I'd be more worried about my ears if I was you.'

'What's wrong with my ears?'

I.C. gasped. 'You mean you don't *know*? They're *massive*!'

I looked past the boy and up to Mr Mumbles. My old imaginary friend glared down at me, and I couldn't quite decide if my day had just got better or worse. Finally, he reached out a hand. I stared at it for a few seconds, like I'd never seen one before. Then I took hold of it and he yanked me smoothly to my feet.

'Thanks,' I said.

'Thank him, not me,' Mumbles growled. He pointed to his throat. 'You've got something there.'

I felt for my own throat and realised that the frozen hand of Doc Mortis was still gripping on. I yanked it off and threw it to the floor, where it broke into several sharp shards.

'So, just to be sure now,' I said, 'he's really dead this time?'

Mumbles prodded some of the broken fragments with his foot. 'Don't see him getting up from that, do you?'

'The way things have been going lately? I'm not going to rule it out. Besides, you were just a pile of dust at one point, and here you are now.'

I.C. wrapped his arms round my waist and hugged me tightly. I could feel the cold emanating from him, but he was beginning to warm up.

'I didn't think I'd see you again,' he said.

'Come on, I promised you you would,' I replied.

'Yeah, but Big Nose said you were a... what was it again? A back-stabbing weasel, that was it.'

'He did, did he?'

Mr Mumbles stared at me impassively. Or, at least, he tried to, but there was a hint of a smirk at the corners of his scarred mouth.

'You're not really a back-stabbing weasel, though, are you?'

'No,' I assured him. 'I'm not.'

I.C. sighed with relief. 'Good.' His brow furrowed. 'What's a weasel, anyway?'

'An animal. A bit like a stoat.'

I.C. gasped. 'Like a *boat*?'

'No, like a stoat.'

'Oh, right. What's a stoat?'

'I'll explain later,' I said.

I.C. finally stepped back and I turned to Mr Mumbles. 'The barrier's gone.'

'I noticed.'

'It's my fault. My dad tricked me.'

Mumbles nodded. 'I tried to warn you.'

'Everyone's dying.'

'Everyone does.'

'But not like this,' I protested. 'They shouldn't die like this. None of this should be happening.'

'But it is happening,' Mumbles said.

'How can I stop it? How can I fix this?'

'I don't know. I don't think you can.'

I had to lean on the wall to stop myself slumping to the floor. I'd already guessed it was too late to stop my dad's plan, but having it confirmed still hit me like a hammer blow.

Was this really it? Was this what the world would be like from now on? Monsters and horror and death at every turn?

'I bet you're loving this, aren't you?' I snapped. I was angry with myself, but Mumbles was a much easier target. 'I bet you're loving being out of the Darkest Corners. Being free.'

'Free?' Mumbles growled. 'How am I free? It wasn't the place that was the problem, it was the things that lived there. But they're all over here too.' He shoved me towards a window and gestured down at the town. Flames had very nearly consumed it completely. Even from this distance, through the glass, I could hear the screams of the dying. 'I didn't escape the Darkest Corners. The Darkest Corners is here with me.'

I watched the fire dancing until I couldn't watch it any longer. 'What am I going to do?' I croaked.

'What do you want to do?'

'I want to find my dad,' I said. 'And I want to kill him.'

Mumbles tugged the rim of his hat, pulling it lower on his head. 'I could get behind that.'

'What? You mean you'll help me? Why?'

'He messed with my head too, remember?' Mumbles said. He jabbed a thumb towards I.C. 'Besides, he'd never let me hear the end of it if I didn't.'

I.C. grinned broadly. He reached a hand up towards Mumbles. The man in the hat hesitated, looked a little embarrassed, then took I.C.'s hand in his.

'How did you two find me, anyway?' I asked as we headed for the exit.

'Luck. We were after Mortis. Didn't know you'd be here.'

'Right. Well that *was* some good luck then.'

Mumbles grunted. 'Who said it was *good* luck?'

We stepped round the broken bodies of the porters outside the cupboard. 'Was that you?' I asked.

Mumbles nodded. 'They weren't the only ones. There were a dozen of them in here when we arrived.'

'Really?' I whispered, suddenly alert.

'*Were*. Past tense.'

'Oh,' I said. 'Um... well done.'

'Never get tired of killing those things.'

I glanced down at I.C., who was two knuckles deep in a nose pick. 'Right. Good,' I said, as brightly as I could manage. 'Shall we go?'

Ameena jumped out from inside the 4x4 as we approached. Her face lit up when she spotted me, then fell when she realised I wasn't alone. When she spotted that one of my companions was Mr Mumbles, she looked ready to jump back in the car and speed away.

'Relax,' I said. 'He's on our side.'

Ameena didn't look convinced, but she didn't make a run for it, either. She shifted her gaze to I.C. and he smiled broadly up at her.

'Hello,' he chirped.

'Uh, hi. You're the ice kid I've heard so much about?'

'That's me!' he said proudly. 'And this is Uncle Mumbles.'

'*Uncle—?*' I began, but Mr Mumbles stared daggers at me.

'Shut it.'

'They've already met,' I told I.C. 'She broke a baseball bat across his face.'

'It's OK, his nose would have blocked it,' I.C. said, then he jumped sideways to avoid a dunt from Mumbles.

'How's Billy?' I asked. I could see him sitting in the back of the car. His eyes were staring straight ahead as his fingers prodded at the stitches in his lips.

'Well, he's not his usual chatty self,' Ameena said. 'Tried to find something to cut the stitches, but no luck.'

I handed her a scalpel. 'Try this. Grabbed it when Doc was on top of me. Was going to use it, but I.C. took care of him before I had to.'

'Give it to me,' Mumbles said. He took the knife and wiped some frost from the blade. 'I'll do it.'

'Is that a good idea?' Ameena asked. 'He's already pretty freaked out. Having you come at him with a scalpel might—'

'I'll do it,' Mumbles growled, and Ameena didn't argue any more.

We climbed into the car, Ameena and me in the front, Billy sandwiched between Mumbles and I.C. in the back. He didn't freak out like I expected him to – and like I probably would've in the same situation – but he did shoot me a worried look.

'Hello, I'm I.C., what's your name?'

For obvious reasons, he didn't get a reply.

'He's Billy,' I said. 'Billy, I.C. and Mr Mumbles.'

Billy let out a high-pitched groan when he saw the scalpel. 'Relax, kid,' Mumbles said. 'I know what I'm doing.'

I could feel everyone in the car holding their breath as Mumbles leaned in with the blade. Everyone expect I.C., who was quietly singing a song. I didn't catch many of the words, but from what I could gather it was about Mr Mumbles' nose, and the sheer size of it.

Mumbles clamped one hand on the top of Billy's head, and brought the blade closer to the stitches. Billy closed his eyes and did his best to control his shaking. Mumbles breathed out, then held it. Then he placed the razor-sharp steel against the first stitch.

'Careful,' I said, and everyone jumped.

Mr Mumbles scowled at me, then tried again. I didn't interrupt this time. The blade tugged. Billy whimpered. And then the first stitch popped loose.

'Drive,' Mumbles said. 'The rest should be easy.'

'Shouldn't we wait until they're all done?' I asked. Billy tried to nod, but the hand on his head held him steady.

'The rest should be easy. Drive.'

Ameena looked to me for guidance. I shrugged, and she fired up the car. 'Where to?'

'Wherever my dad is.'

'I don't know. He didn't tell me where he was going. I ran away before I found out.'

I leaned round to Mumbles. 'Any ideas?'

'Here's one: shut up and let me concentrate.' Another stitch was sliced open and Billy's lips loosened a little.

'You sure you don't know?' I asked Ameena. 'He didn't even give any hints?'

'No, he never really told me anything. Bump coming!'

Mumbles pulled the scalpel away from Billy as the 4x4 bounced back down on to the road.

'Great, so he could be anywhere,' I sighed.

'Yeah. Except...'

'Except what?'

'Except I think he'd want to rub it in. You know? That he's won. He knew he could never really escape the Darkest Corners. He knew he could never get back to the real world the way it was. That wasn't the reason he was really doing any of this.'

'He wanted to hurt me,' I said, my voice hushed. 'He told me he was doing all this just so he could hurt me. He wanted me to bring the Darkest Corners here so I'd have all this death on my conscience.'

'Exactly. And I reckon he'd want to revel in that. He'd go somewhere that'd always remind him that he won. Somewhere he could gloat.'

'Can't you sniff him out?' I.C. suggested. 'You know, with your big nose?'

Mumbles sighed. 'No.'

'Really?' I.C. gasped. 'I thought you'd be able to smell *Australia* with that thing!'

Mumbles snapped back at him, but I wasn't paying any attention now. I was thinking about his and Ameena's words. Somewhere that would remind him he'd won. Somewhere he could gloat.

It hit me then. Somewhere that would break my heart.

'Home,' I said, and my voice cracked with the weight of the word. 'Take me home.'

Chapter Fifteen

HELLO THERE, MR SQUIRREL

By the time we were halfway to the village, Billy's mouth was open. Fresh blood seeped from the holes above and below his lips, and the stitches lay scattered across the floor in the back of the car.

Mumbles was sitting back in his seat now. He looked cartoonishly large, squashed in, his head touching the roof.

'Thanks,' Billy said, wiping the worst of the blood on his sleeve.

'No problem,' Mumbles shrugged. 'Stings for a while, but you get over it.'

Billy nodded. 'Thanks,' he said again. He tried a smile, but it clearly hurt too much for him to quite pull it off.

The car's occupants fell silent after that, save for I.C.

singing softly about the scale of Mr Mumbles' facial features.

It was Billy who eventually spoke. His throat was dry, making him hard to hear over the sound of the 4x4's engine.

'Why's she here?'

He was staring at the back of Ameena's head, looking almost like the bully he used to be.

'She's OK,' I said. 'She's on our side. It was all just –' I glanced across at the girl in the driving seat – 'a misunderstanding.'

Billy didn't seem satisfied with this answer, but he didn't press the issue. 'So... what happened? To the world, I mean.'

All eyes went to me for the reply.

'It was my fault,' I said. 'My dad tricked me into using my abilities. I brought the barrier down, and now everyone's dying.'

'You can stop it, right?'

I didn't answer.

'But, your magic power thing. The stuff you can do. You can stop it. I mean, you've *got* to stop it.'

'I can't do any of that any more,' I said. 'It doesn't work in the Darkest Corners, and the Darkest Corners is now here.'

Billy leaned back and looked out through the windows. We were approaching the village again and the sounds of madness and chaos were already reaching out to meet us.

'So, what, everyone dies? That's it?'

'Pretty much,' Ameena said. 'And it wasn't your fault, Kyle.'

I looked at her. 'It was.'

'No, it really wasn't. He'd been planning this for years. He had all kinds of back-up ideas figured out. He would just have kept coming after you until you eventually broke. He was actually impressed you lasted as long as you did, but he would never have given up. One way or another, he'd have worn you down.'

'She's right,' Mumbles said. 'He thought I'd be enough

to get you to open the gateway, and look what happened there. You coped with everything he threw at you. In the end, he had to resort to tricking you. He didn't break you. You broke *him*.'

I gritted my teeth and stared ahead through the windscreen. 'Not yet. But I'm going to.'

'He'll be well protected,' Ameena said. 'He built up a loyal following over there. You won't just be fighting him, you'll be fighting an army.'

'If that's what it takes,' I said. 'But I don't expect any of you to come with me if you don't want to. This is my fight now.'

'You're kidding, right?' Ameena said. 'I'm coming with you.'

'Me too,' Billy added.

'We could all get killed.'

'Yeah, well,' Billy shrugged. 'Whatever. What's left to live for, anyway?'

'That's the spirit, Bill,' Ameena cheered.

'Mumbles?' I said.

'I'm in.'

'What about I.C.? Won't it be too dangerous?'

'He can handle himself. I've been training him.'

'Yeah, but for what? A fortnight?'

'He's a fast learner.'

'Super fast. Zoom zoom!' I.C. added, then he reached round the back of my chair and gave me a pat on the head.

'I dunno. We should probably get him somewhere safe.'

'Where do you suggest?' Mumbles asked, and there was no real answer to that.

'I want to come. Want to help,' I.C. insisted.

I realised in that moment that I had something I had never had before. I had friends. Real friends, who were prepared to stand by me, whatever the cost.

Oh, sure, one of them was a borderline teenage psychopath who used to beat me on a daily basis, and the other three didn't technically exist, but I never said they were perfect.

'Thank you,' I told them. 'But we're not taking I.C. in there. It's too dangerous.'

Before anyone could reply, a *roar* from overhead made everyone but Mr Mumbles duck.

A fighter jet screamed above us through the darkened sky. 'Hairyplane!' I.C. cried, and he banged his head off the window while trying to get a better look.

'The air force,' Billy cried. 'They're sending in the military. It's going to be OK.'

I almost laughed with relief. Not because I thought the jet would swoop down and save us, but because it meant we weren't alone. With what I'd seen on TV and what I'd seen up close, it had begun to feel like Billy and I were the only real people left. But we weren't. There were others. At least one.

I watched the jet bank sharply to the left. Then I noticed that there was something else flying close beside it, virtually invisible in the dark. It looked to be black or charcoal grey, with dragon-like wings and a long, whip-like tail.

The jet levelled off and the black shape closed in. Its wings were spread out, mirroring those of the jet. It glided above the plane, then dropped down and clung on like a limpet. I could almost hear the pilot's screams of confusion and fear.

'It's going down,' Ameena said.

'Pull up,' I whispered. 'Pull up, pull up, pull up!'

But a moment later the sky was lit up by a ball of orange flame as the plane struck the hillside. Ameena slammed on the brakes, dazzled by the sudden light. We watched the flames licking over the grass and saw the smoke curling lazily into the air.

'He ejected,' I said, fooling no one. 'He ejected and got out.'

'No, he didn't,' Mumbles grunted.

'We don't know that,' Ameena interjected. 'Maybe Kyle's right. Maybe...' But she couldn't think of a convincing argument.

'He could've saved us,' Billy croaked. 'It might have been OK.'

'No, it wouldn't,' I said, with more venom than I should have. 'The whole world's affected, Billy. There are billions of the things flooding every town and city on Earth. How was one plane going to help?'

The car gave a violent shudder. The engine spluttered. Ameena stared at the dashboard as all the little warning icons lit up like a Christmas tree.

'What now?' I asked.

'I have no idea.' Ameena turned the key. The engine rumbled for a few moments, then died away completely. When she turned the key again, the car didn't make a sound. 'Dead. It's completely dead.'

Billy leaned forward. 'What? How?'

'I don't know, Billy! It just died.'

'You've done something, haven't you?' Billy snapped. 'You've done something. Start it up again. You're doing this on purpose!'

'Of course I'm not doing it on purpose.'

I looked at her. 'To be fair, it is the sort of thing you'd think was funny.'

'Well,' she said thoughtfully. 'Yes, that's true, but I didn't do anything. The car won't start.'

'What will we do?' I.C. asked from the back.

'It's not far from here,' I said. 'A couple more bends and we're there.'

'A couple more bends in the dark,' Billy added.

'Not scared of the dark, are you?' Ameena snapped.

'No, I'm scared of what might be hiding *in* the dark waiting to kill me. Which at this point is probably everything.'

'There's no choice,' I told him. I looked around the car. There were trees on one side, a rocky slope leading steeply upwards on the other. Driving, it would've been two minutes maximum until we reached the edge of the village. On foot it would be more like ten. I opened my door. 'We'll have to make a run for it.'

There was a cackle from down near the ground. I looked in time to see something the size of a small monkey come scrabbling up through my half-open door. Its movements were monkey-like too. It swung up the door, bounced on my lap, then propelled itself directly towards my face. I ducked to the side, then heard Billy cry out in panic.

'*Getitoffgetitoffgetitoff!*'

Ameena and I spun in our seats. The thing was clinging on to Billy's face, its hands and feet holding on to clumps of his hair. It was completely bald, with raw-looking pink skin covering it from head to toe. Its face was squashed up like a bat, and its pointed ears flapped as it sniggered with delight.

'Hold still,' Mumbles growled. He clamped a hand across the thing's bony back and pulled. There was a sudden tearing sound and the creature let out a short, sharp squeal.

The thing kept holding on to Billy's head, but now there was one in Mumbles' hand too. It blinked rapidly, had a quick check of its bearings, then shot up Mumbles' sleeve. He punched his forearm furiously, trying to flatten the bulge that was now moving up towards his elbow.

Just as the bulge neared his bicep, a fist smashed down on it. Direct hit. There was a squelchy cracking sound and the lump stopped moving.

A second later, two mounds began making their way along the sleeve in opposite directions. From beneath the coat I could hear both creatures snigger. The one on Billy's face was still holding on, giggling hysterically as it ground its raw flesh across his cheeks.

'There's things in here!' I.C. announced.

'We seem them, it's OK,' I said.

'I think they're squirrels. Hello there, Mr Squirrel.' I.C. reached over to pat the thing on Billy's face. It hissed and nipped at his fingers with little sharp teeth. I.C. gave a high-pitched '*Eek!*' and jumped back. 'I don't think they're squirrels,' he decided.

Mr Mumbles was thrashing about on the seat now, punching and slapping four mounds that moved around below his coat. Billy was trying to pull the thing off his face, but whenever his hands got near, it would snap at him, then laugh when he pulled away.

'What are they?' I asked.

'Little Nasties,' Ameena replied.

'I see that, but what are they?'

'No, they're Little Nasties. That's what we call them. Came across a whole community of them a few years back. Wasn't much fun. This one must've done something to the underside of the car. That's why it died. That's what they're like – not dangerous, just annoying.'

Billy yelped as the Little Nasty on his face took a bite out of the top of his finger.

'OK, so they're a *bit* dangerous,' Ameena said.

'Stop discussing it,' Billy yelped. 'Get rid of it!'

Ameena shrugged. 'They usually just get bored and wander off.'

Billy tugged on the creature. It gave a soft *pop* and another one came away in his hands.

'Oh yeah, and they're unstable. Physically, I mean. Although probably emotionally too, if you really wanted to analyse them. They self-replicate when they get injured.' She glanced at Mr Mumbles, who was now thrashing and kicking wildly at a swarm of lumps moving beneath his coat. 'Probably should've mentioned that sooner, really.'

Mumbles arched his back and tore open his coat. The buttons pinged off the roof and windows, and then the inside of the 4x4 was filled with a dozen or more of the bare-skinned beasts. They leapt across the back of the seats, scrambling through hair and over shoulders and across the controls of the car.

I lashed out, knocking them away, but every time I hit one, it became two. 'Everybody out,' I barked, rolling through my open door and on to the road. I heard the driver's door open and Ameena jumped down. We both ran towards the front of the car, swiping at the Little Nasties that had clung to us through our escape.

I felt one gripping on to my back, right in the middle of my spine. Another clambered up my shoulder and chittered madly in my ear. Ameena grabbed them both, held them by the legs, then tossed them into the trees. They howled as they sailed through the air, then landed with a rustle somewhere in the leaves.

We spent a few seconds checking one another over, then looked back at the 4x4. The front doors stood open, but Billy, Mumbles and I.C. were still sitting in the back. The car rocked violently on its wheels as all three of them flapped wildly at the Nasties.

'Why don't they just get out?' I wondered.

'No idea,' Ameena shrugged, then she put a hand over her mouth. 'Oh, wait. Police car. You can't open the back doors from the inside.'

I felt the blood drain from my face, but couldn't stop a nervous giggle rising in my stomach. 'They're going to kill us.'

Ameena grinned, making her nose wrinkle up. 'We should probably go and open the doors.'

There was a sharp screeching of metal, then, that made us both jump back. The rear door on the driver's side buckled and flew away from the car.

'Or not,' I said.

Mr Mumbles stumbled out of the car, twisting and bucking like a drunken dad dancing at a wedding.

Billy tumbled out next, the first Nasty still attached to his face. There were at least five others now scampering around his upper body, but it was too dark and they were moving too fast to count them accurately.

'Can't... breathe,' Billy gasped. The one on his face had flattened its torso across his mouth and nose. It cackled gleefully as it smothered him.

He tried to prise the Nasty away, but its teeth nipped his finger again and again. I hurried over to help, but three of the things were suddenly scampering up my legs.

Mr Mumbles was heaving with Nasties now. They covered him from head to toe, inside his clothes and out. One perched on the top of his hat, hungrily chewing the brim. He swung a hand up and punched it off, and five more landed on the road beside him.

I turned to Ameena, but she was struggling with a small army of the things. Removing them gently was impossible because of those teeth, and any sudden movements just made more of them.

As another few of them landed on my back, I began to panic. Billy was on his knees. Mr Mumbles was standing, but only just. Ameena had said the Little Nasties would get bored and wander off, but when? And what if they didn't? Was this it? Was it really going to end like this?

A blast of chill air hit me, almost freezing the breath in my lungs. I.C. stood inside the car, his head and shoulders sticking out through the sunroof. He had his arms raised, his eyes closed, and his tongue was sticking out from the corner of his mouth in concentration.

'Everyone stand still, please,' he said, and icy vapour swirled from his mouth. 'But not you, Mr Squirrel,' he added as an afterthought.

All four of us did our best to stop moving. Even Mumbles, who now had hundreds of the critters climbing over him. The Nasties that were scampering across me twittered anxiously. I felt their body temperature drop, and saw their pink skin become white, then blue.

Where they touched my own bare flesh, it began to sting. The pain was sharp and sudden, and then it was gone. One by one, the Little Nasties fell off and landed like freakishly large hailstones on the road.

It took several long moments for us to grasp what had

happened, and to accept that the Nasties weren't getting back up. Ever.

I looked over to I.C., who was beaming proudly at each of us in turn. 'OK,' I said to Mumbles, who was shaking frozen rodent-monsters out through the bottoms of his trouser legs. 'He can come.'

Chapter Sixteen

THE LONG WALK

Ameena and I took the front. Mumbles and I.C. followed at the back, with Billy walking between us. I'd grabbed the police baton, and Ameena had taken hers. They would be useless against any more Little Nasties, but they could do some damage to anything else we might encounter.

As long as it wasn't too big. Or armoured. Or equipped with any sort of projectile weapon. Or reasonably fast-moving.

Or just very determined.

I looked down at the telescopic baton. Not for the first time, I wished it was a shotgun.

It was a long walk back to the village. The only light

was the glow of the fire on the hillside where the plane had come down, and that was barely enough to let us see the road directly in front of us.

The January wind curled around us as we walked, bringing with it the smell of smoke and a light swirl of dusty ash. Everyone but I.C. and Mr Mumbles shivered in the cold.

We hadn't spoken for several minutes, and the silence was letting doubts creep into my head. The village had been a warzone before the barrier had come down. What chance did we have of getting through it now?

I tried to make conversation, just to take my mind off my fears. 'At least there's no snow. The place was covered in it earlier.'

'I did that!'

I turned back to look at I.C., but could barely make him out in the dark. 'You did? Why?'

'Damage control,' Mumbles said. 'We found out your dad was planning to send the girl through.'

'Rosie?'

'Don't know, don't care. I just knew what she could do. That she'd infect people.'

'So you tried to contain them,' I said. 'You really made all that snow?'

'Yeppy-doodle!'

'Wow,' I said with a low whistle. I was impressed. When I'd left I.C. he had no control over his abilities whatsoever. They only kicked in when he was in fear of his life, and even then they were unpredictable. Two weeks with Mr Mumbles and he was capable of snowing in an entire village. What would he be like after a month?

But we'd never know. We'd never know what he'd be like after a month, two months, a year. Tonight was the night we were almost certainly all going to die, just like my mum, Joseph and the others.

Actually, that was a point.

'There was a guy helping me,' I said to Mumbles. 'His name was Joseph.'

'So?'

'I don't know who he was.'

'How should I know?'

'I... I don't know. I think he was from the Darkest Corners. He was balding, about – I dunno – fifty or sixty, maybe?'

Mumbles shrugged. 'Not a clue.'

'He was the cop you punched through the glass door of the police station when you were trying to kill us,' Ameena added.

'Oh yeah, forgot about that,' I said. I looked back at Mumbles. 'Ringing any bells?'

'I didn't punch him, I threw him.'

'Well, that's not so bad then,' Ameena said.

'So you remember him?' I asked.

Mumbles shook his head. 'Wasn't really paying much attention.'

'Oh,' I said, disappointed. We walked the rest of the way in silence.

It took longer than we expected – twenty minutes, maybe more – before we finally arrived at the outskirts of the village. It wasn't a big place: from the first building to my house was really just four or five streets. Of course, those four or five streets would be populated by screechers and worse, so it wouldn't be easy.

Or so I thought.

'It's quiet,' Ameena whispered. She was leaning round the corner of a fence and peering along the first road. Flames flickered in cars and in the windows of several houses, but the fire damage wasn't nearly as bad here as it had looked in the town.

'Almost too—' I.C. began, but the rest of us cut him off in unison.

'Don't say it!'

He looked up at us with solemn eyes. 'You folks are crazy.'

'Where have they gone?' I wondered. 'The whole place was heaving with them.'

'Maybe they've run away,' Billy suggested.

'I hope not,' I said. 'Because then I'd have to ask "From what?" and I probably wouldn't want to know the answer.'

'From us, maybe?' he said.

Mumbles snorted. 'Fat chance. They'd look at us and see lunch. My guess is the plane exploding on the hill drew a lot of them away.'

'That was lucky,' Ameena said.

'Tell that to the pilot,' I replied.

Mr Mumbles picked I.C. up with one hand and hoisted the boy on to his shoulder. 'Thanks, Big Nose,' I.C. said, then he leaned over, pushed in Mumbles' nose and said, 'Honk.'

'We should move now,' Mumbles barked, and it sounded like an order, not a suggestion. 'Before they come back.'

'Right,' I agreed. I looked to the others. 'Ready then?'

There were no wisecracks, no complaints. Billy and Ameena just nodded.

I crept out past the fence, leading the others in single file. It would be quicker to take the short cuts through the alleyways behind the houses, but they were too narrow and we could be trapped too easily. The streets themselves, even though they were much more exposed, would be the safest route.

I hoped.

We walked quickly, crouched low, our heads constantly moving as we scanned for danger. The streets weren't just empty, they were virtually silent too. The only sounds were the crackling of the fires we passed, and the scuffing of our shoes on the pavement.

Which is why I almost jumped out of my skin when Billy spoke. 'I want you to know. I'm sorry,' he said. His throat was still dry and his ragged lips made him slur his words. It took me half a second to process what he'd said.

'What for?'

'Just, you know? Being a massive git for all those years.'

I hesitated. 'Don't worry about it. You weren't.'

'He so was,' Ameena said.

'She's right. I was. And I'm sorry.'

'It's fine,' I said to the boy who had made most of my

childhood a misery. 'Everything's changed. None of us are who we were six weeks ago.'

KAAAAAWRK.

I stopped and ducked. A bird. *A crow.* I'd heard a crow! We all crouched down in the shadow of the fence, our eyes searching the darkness above us.

'Can't see it,' I whispered. 'Anyone?'

'I got it,' Ameena whispered.

'Where?'

Her hand passed my cheek and pointed to the top of a telegraph pole ten or so metres along the street. A fat black bird sat there, barely visible in the low light.

KAAAAAAWRK.

It was impossible to know if the bird had seen us or not. It was perched along the route I had planned to take us, though, so even if it hadn't seen us yet, it would do soon enough.

'We should turn back,' I suggested. 'Try to find another way.'

'What if the rest of them come back, though?' Ameena asked. 'We need to keep moving.'

'Any suggestions on how we deal with that then?' I asked, staring pointedly at the bird.

There was a muffled *snap* behind me as Mumbles broke a strip off the bottom of the fence. He set I.C. down on the ground, then stood up. His arm drew back. I heard a faint *whistle* sound as the jagged wood shot like a javelin through the air.

The bird started to let out another squawk, just as the wood pierced its head. Its wings opened and twitched frantically for a second or less, then it fell with a *thump* on to the road far below.

'Right then,' Mumbles muttered, lifting I.C. back on to his shoulder. 'Let's go get this over with.'

My house was lit up blindingly bright when we turned the final corner. My heart leapt into my throat at the sight of it. For a moment I thought it was burning, but I soon realised I was wrong.

Every light in the house was on, from the living room to the upstairs bathroom. The rest of the power in the village seemed to be out, so the house stood out like a beacon against the near-darkness.

'See?' Ameena said. 'He's gloating.'

'My house. He's in my house.' I felt my hands begin to shake. 'He's... he's really in my house.'

'It's not too late, you know?' she said, her dark eyes fixing on mine. 'We can still run. We can get away. Together.'

'Trying to protect him, are you?' I snapped. She blinked, but didn't look away.

'Trying to protect *you*. I don't want you to die, Kyle. I don't want him to hurt you any more.'

'My house,' I growled, turning away from her. 'He's in my house.'

'Easy. Don't let it upset you,' Mumbles said. He put a hand on my shoulder, but I shrugged it off.

'I'm way past "upset".'

It was a two-hundred-metre walk uphill to the house. I

set off walking quickly, then found myself breaking into a run. The thought of him there, sitting in the home I'd shared with my mum, made adrenaline surge through my veins and rage fill up what was left of me. I raced on, the pain in my knee all but forgotten.

'Wait!'

That was Mr Mumbles' voice, low and urgent. I ignored it and kept running. The man who had ruined not just my life, but the entire world, was in there somewhere in my home. Sitting on my mum's bed, maybe, or looking in her wardrobe, or finding some other way to trample all over her memory.

'Kyle, stop!'

That was Ameena, not as close behind me as I'd have expected. Too scared to run, probably. Too afraid of facing the man – *the monster* – who had used her to get to me. I was scared, too, but it was a fear that drove me on, not held me back. It was the fear of *not* getting to him, *not* facing him, *not* making him pay. I would not, *could not*, fail. Not this time.

'It's a trap!'

That was Ameena too, shrill and more panicked than I'd ever heard her. *A trap*. I allowed myself a grim smile. Of course it was a trap. I knew it was a trap.

I just didn't care.

The first one bounded over a fence a little ahead of me on the right. It was short and gloopy-looking, with long stringy strands of something like seaweed trailing from its limbs.

The smell of it reached me first. It was the smell of week-old fish. The thing itself followed close behind, arms reaching out, slimy face contorted in a snarl.

I ducked the arms, turned sharply and smashed the baton into the creature's ribs. It gave a bubbly shriek and tried to turn. I swung with the baton again, smashing it against the back of its thigh this time. It went down with a *splat* and I set off running once more towards the house.

I could see the rest of them now. Things of all shapes and sizes emerged from cover along the road. They were ahead of me, behind me, drawing in from both sides.

Hairy things, scaly things, things with no real texture at all. They closed in, cutting me off from Ameena and the others.

'Come on then!' I bellowed, and some of them actually seemed to hesitate.

Most didn't, though. I heard a clicking on the pavement and turned in time for something small and fast-moving to launch itself at my chest. I hit the road hard and the baton rolled from my hand.

The thing on my chest began to claw at my shirt, snarling and spitting like something demonic. I made a grab for it and my fingers found damp fur. It raised its head and flashed its jagged teeth. I spotted its plush nose and little red bow tie and in that moment I realised I was fighting a teddy bear.

Ignoring the teeth, I clamped a hand down on its head and pulled. The synthetic fur stretched. A seam split. The teddy howled as its stuffing spilled out on to the street.

And then it stopped howling. I tossed the empty skin away, grabbed the baton and leapt back to my feet in time to see an entire army of monsters slowly closing in around me.

I turned on the spot, baton ready. How many of them were there? Dozens? Hundreds? I couldn't tell. They swarmed from every direction, filling the whole street. They looked like exhibits in some weird alien zoo, a few of them vaguely human-looking, but most of them too bizarre for words.

Eyes trained on me. Tongues flicked hungrily across bloated lips. Knuckles cracked and muscles twitched and on they came, closer and closer, nearer and nearer.

'Stop.'

I recognised the voice. That was him. My dad. My head snapped up at the sound of his voice. He leaned on the ledge of my open bedroom window, looking down. At his command the circle of horror stopped closing in. He smiled at that, enjoying the power.

'Leave him. He's mine.'

A disappointed murmur rippled around the crowd. It parted just enough for Ameena and the others to be shoved through. Billy stumbled, but I caught him before he could hit the ground. He looked like he wanted to cry, but he was doing his damnedest not to.

'As we were saying,' Mumbles scowled. '"Look out, it's a trap."'

A girl with her hair scraped back in a tight ponytail and blood across her face stepped forward. She looked to be about ten years old until she scowled, revealing teeth that had been filed to razor-sharp points. 'What about the rest of them? What do we do with his friends?'

My dad tapped his chin. 'Well... sorry, what was your name?'

The girl cracked her knuckles. 'Leah,' she said. 'Leah Wilson.'

'Oh,' said my dad flatly. 'Really? I expected something scarier. Never mind. Well, Leah Wilson, here's what I suggest.' A crooked smile parted his lips. 'Kill them. Kill them all.' He fixed me with eyes filled with glee. 'And be sure to do it slowly.'

Mr Mumbles snorted out a laugh. He jabbed a thumb

in the direction of the little girl. 'What, Tinkerbell? Kill *me*? I'd like to see her try.'

Leah Wilson flicked her wrists. A long curved claw erupted through the flesh on the back of each hand and she let out an animal hiss.

'OK,' said Mumbles, suddenly sounding much less confident, 'maybe I wouldn't.'

Chapter Seventeen

RING OF DEATH

Led by Leah Wilson, the crowd began to edge towards us. We all drew together in the centre of the circle. 'Any ideas?'

'Don't go running along the street like a mental patient?' Ameena suggested. 'Oh wait, too late.'

Up on Mr Mumbles' shoulder, I.C. whimpered. Something bald and wrinkly lumbered a few paces forward and made a grab for the boy's dangling feet. Mumbles raised a foot and kicked the thing in the groin, then drove a fist into the back of its head as it doubled over in pain. Its nose burst noisily as its face hit the tarmac.

'Ready?' asked the man in the hat.

I.C. nodded. 'Sure am, Uncle Mumbles.'

Mumbles grabbed hold of I.C.'s ankles. 'Please — call me Big Nose,' he said, then he glanced at me and the others. 'On the ground. Now.'

We dropped down into the push-up position just as Mumbles began to spin. I.C. squealed as he was flung outwards, Mumbles holding his feet as he turned faster and faster on the spot.

Frost began to flow from I.C.'s fingers. It swirled like a tornado as Mumbles continued to spin, and I felt it chill my back as it rolled across the crowd.

The girl with the claws lunged, but immediately froze solid, her face still fixed in that animal snarl. The rest of the front row quickly began to frost over. Those behind, realising what was happening, began pushing into the next row back. Within moments the first fight broke out as something large bumped into something larger.

The night was split by a chorus of squeals and roars as fists and feet and claws began to fly. The army was turning on itself, even as the cloud of cold spread through its ranks.

'We'll hold them,' Mumbles barked. 'You lot go get *him*.'

I looked up to my dad and saw he was no longer leaning casually on the window ledge. He was standing straight, the smile falling from his face.

His eyes met mine. He gestured down at the front door just as it swung inwards. 'Come on in, son,' he said. 'Welcome home.'

I jumped up and started to run, dodging through horrific ice sculptures on my way to the door. Ameena caught me by the arm. 'Take it easy,' she warned. 'Be careful. It's bound to be another trap.'

Billy stepped up beside me. 'But don't worry. We've got your back.'

'Thanks,' I said, then I handed him the baton. 'Take this.'

'What? Why?'

'You're better at beating people up than I am.'

He hesitated. 'Was that a dig?'

'Yes. No. Maybe.' I gave a sigh. 'I don't even know any more.'

'Just get a bloody move on!' Mumbles roared, his shout shoving us on into the house.

I stopped again just inside the front door, overwhelmed by the feeling of being back home, and the knowledge that this might well be the last time I ever would be.

The living room was trashed – even more so than the last time I'd seen it. The furniture was upturned or broken. The TV was smashed, the wallpaper was torn and the smear of blood the Beast had left across the ceiling had dried to a dark, dirty red.

More blood pooled on the patch of carpet where we'd found the dead policewoman, who'd turned out not to be nearly as dead as she looked. That had been what? A day ago? Two? A lifetime of horror had happened since then.

'Come up, come up, don't be shy,' called my dad from upstairs.

I heard Ameena say, 'This is it,' but my legs were already carrying me towards the stairs. I walked up slowly, expecting him or something else to appear at the top, but no one did.

Billy and Ameena stuck close behind me. We stopped at my bedroom door. My heart was racing, pounding like a hammer against the inside of my chest. My knee throbbed in time with my pulse – *boom-boom-boom-boom* – as I nudged open the door to my room.

Empty. He wasn't there.

I looked at the window, which still stood open. A few weeks ago Mr Mumbles had tapped against it, trying to get inside so he could kill me. How things had changed.

Further along the landing, I heard a door open. I knew without looking which door it was. My fists clenched and my jaw tensed. My mum's bedroom. He was in Mum's bedroom.

'There you are,' he said when I stepped out of my room. 'And you've brought your little school friend too, I see. How nice.' He flicked his gaze across at Ameena and I felt her wilt behind me. 'And as for you,' he said. 'Well, we'll get to you later.'

I took a step towards him and he held up a hand. 'Wait!' he said, and to my annoyance I found myself obeying. 'It's three against one. That's not fair.'

'It's just me and you,' I told him. He laughed, a big deep hollow laugh that reminded me how much bigger than me he was.

'No, I don't think so. Your little friends would jump in at the first chance they got.' His eyes gleamed. 'Unless, of course, I could find some way of keeping them occupied.'

He looked very deliberately at the door across the landing from mine. It was the bedroom my nan used to sleep in before she went to the home. Ameena had slept there too, after my mum invited her to stay.

The door was closed now. A slide-bolt lock, like the kind you sometimes find on gates and sheds, had been fastened to the door. The bolt was in the closed position, making it impossible to open from the inside.

'Not bad, eh?' my dad said. 'I mean, I'm no carpenter, but not too shabby a job, if I do say so myself.'

'Why did you do that?' I asked. 'What's in there?'

'Take a look.'

'No.'

'Aaaah,' he said, waggling a finger, 'but I wasn't talking to you. I was talking to *you*, Billy.'

Billy's acne-scarred brow furrowed. 'Me?'

'That's right. You.' He gestured towards the door. 'Take a look. I think you'll find it very interesting.'

Billy stared at the door.

'Don't do it,' I told him. His head twitched and he looked away.

'What, you think I'm an idiot? Of course I won't.'

The lopsided grin spread across my dad's face. He hooked his thumbs into the belt loops of his jeans and leaned against the doorframe. 'Won't you? I think you will.'

'Well, you're wrong.'

'Really? Bet your life?'

'Don't listen to him, Billy,' Ameena warned. 'He'll mess with your head.'

'Go on. Just a quick look,' my dad urged. 'What harm could it do? Open, closed. Quick peek in, no harm done.'

Billy was focused on the door again, fixated on the

lock. He cocked his head and listened to the sound of footsteps on carpet that now came from inside the room.

'What is that?' he muttered. 'What's in there?'

'What do you think it is?'

Billy scowled. 'How should I know? What is it?'

'You mean *who* is it?'

A terrible quiet fell across the landing.

'No,' I whispered, staring in horror at my father. 'No, don't. You can't.'

'What? What's he on about?' Billy asked. He looked the door up and down and shifted from foot to foot. 'Who is it?'

'Only one way to find out.'

'Don't. Don't do it,' I said.

Billy kept staring at the lock, kept bouncing nervously on the balls of his feet. Tears began to trickle down his bloodied cheeks. He knew. He knew as well as I did who was beyond that door.

'Come on, Billy. She's just dying to see you.'

'Don't listen to him,' Ameena said, but Billy was already grasping for the lock.

'Stop,' I said, grabbing for him. 'Don't open it. It's too late.'

The lock fell to the floor the moment he touched it. My dad laughed again. 'Well, looks like I didn't do so great a job after all.'

'Billy, don't!' I caught his sleeve, but he yanked it away and pushed the handle down.

And there she was, the little girl in the pink pyjamas. The little girl who Billy had abandoned to the screechers when they had first arrived. Billy's baby sister, Lily.

Only it wasn't. Not really. She was merely what remained of Lily.

She had been human, of course, but now she wasn't. Her body was twisted and bent, her knuckles pressed against the floor. Spiky shards of bone stuck out from the knotted muscles across her back and through the few scraps of the pyjamas that still remained.

Her mouth was a ragged cavern of teeth, with strands of saliva hanging like ropes from her wide jaws. Both eyes were a glossy black. I saw Billy reflected in them as he sank to his knees in the doorway and held his arms wide.

'Oh, Lil,' he whimpered. 'I'm sorry.'

'Billy, no!'

I shouldered him out of the way and grabbed for the door handle. Lily lunged, but I hauled the door closed in time to stop her getting free.

'No, no, *no*!' Billy sobbed. 'Let me see her. Let her out.'

Ameena spun him round and drove a right hook across his jaw. Billy dropped like a sack of bricks. I looked down at him, lying unconscious on the floor.

'Good call,' I said.

Ameena shrugged. 'Been looking for an excuse if I'm honest.'

'Oh, come on,' my dad said. 'You spoil all my fun.'

'Fun's over,' I said.

I tried to get to him, tried to reach him, but he raised his hand and I realised he was holding a gun. It was a semi-automatic pistol, if every action movie I'd ever seen was to be believed. I stopped when he levelled the weapon at my head.

'This is the gun that killed your mother. And you're right,

it is all my fault,' he said. 'Thank you for recognising all the hard work I've put in. It makes it all worthwhile. Now stay where you are.' He glanced at Ameena. 'And as for you... Excellent work, my dear. You've done well, bringing him to me.'

I turned to her, my heart rising up into my throat. 'No,' I whispered as her eyes turned to meet mine. 'Please no. Not again.'

Chapter Eighteen

BETRAYED

Ameena looked from me to my dad and back again.
'No,' I said, my voice desperate, pleading, 'but...
no. It's not true. Tell me you didn't.'

'Too trusting, that's your problem,' said my dad. 'Far
too trusting.'

'He's lying,' Ameena said. 'You're lying. I wasn't helping
you. I ran away! Kyle, you've got to believe me, I wasn't
helping him.'

'Well, this is awkward,' my dad said.

I ignored him, kept fixing on Ameena. 'Why?'

'He's lying! I wasn't helping him.'

'Oh, but you were, Ameena,' he said. 'Although... OK.
So maybe you didn't know it.'

We both turned to face him. 'What?'

'I knew you'd go running to him, even after I told you not to. I knew you'd betray me. I knew you'd go running off to his little dream hospital and show him the truth.'

He looked at me. 'Don't you see? I wanted you awake. I wanted you *aware*. I wanted you to come here and face me.'

A huge sense of relief washed over me. Ameena hadn't betrayed me again. She had chosen me over him.

But still, the final bricks of my world were crumbling around me. Ameena had turned against him. She'd tried to get me to run, but instead I had done exactly as he wanted me to do. 'But... why? Why did you want me here?'

'For this, of course! For the final showdown!' he said, then he cackled with glee. 'Oh, sure, I could've just left you lying in your make-believe happy hospital. That would still have been a victory, but where's the drama? Hmm? Where's the sense of closure to it all?'

He ran a hand through his hair and looked me up and

down. 'This – all this – has been years in the planning, kiddo. Over a decade of figuring out the fine detail of how best to make you suffer. Like you made me suffer.'

'I didn't,' I said weakly.

'You were born. That was enough.' His eyes glazed over for a moment as he recalled some distant memory. 'She believed in me, your mother. Really believed. The Bible touched on it, you know? "Faith can move mountains." It's like all the self-help books say – if you believe in something enough, it'll happen. Your mother believed, and I happened.'

He held his arms to the side, showing himself off. I thought about grabbing for the gun, but he moved it back to me before I could make the decision.

'I know that,' I said. 'You told me. She needed you so much you somehow became real, then I came along and she stopped needing you, so you faded away.'

'Was *torn* away,' he seethed. 'Tossed into the Darkest Corners with the rest of them. Left to rot.'

'God. Get over it.'

'Oh, I will. Just as soon as all the loose ends are tied up. It's nearly over, son,' he said, and there was almost kindness in his voice. 'Your friends out there, they'll soon be dead. I'll be honest, I did not foresee Mr Mumbles switching loyalties like that. I send him to kill you and he becomes your guardian angel. Who'd have thought it?' He smiled. 'Still, it all worked out in the end.'

I looked down at the gun. It was fixed on me. Ameena was on the balls of her feet, ready to move, but I caught her sleeve and held her in place.

'You see, I've systematically set about destroying you, son. I've killed the people you care about, I've terrorised you, I've made you a wanted criminal sleeping on the streets and rummaging in bins just to survive.'

His eyes blazed with dark excitement. 'And then there're the abilities you possess. I'd like to say they're all from my side, of course, but that's not true. They come from your unique parentage. A real mother and an imaginary father. The ability to dream, and the power to make those dreams come true. I showed you that power, and then I told you what would happen if you tried to use it.'

He laughed and rocked back on his heels. 'That must've really hurt. All those god-like abilities and you couldn't allow yourself to use them. I don't know how you coped with that.' He put his hand over his mouth. 'Oh, wait, you didn't, did you?'

'You tricked me.'

'And you unleashed Hell on seven billion innocent people.'

'You killed my family!'

He took a step back and pointed the gun at the centre of my chest.

'And now I'm going to kill you. All those years of planning have been leading right to this moment, and it's better than I could've dared hope. Your birth sent me away,' he said, his voice becoming louder, 'and with your death, I am reborn as king of this new world!'

'No, don't! Don't!'

Ameena jumped in front of me. His finger tensed. The

roar of the gun filled the hallway and made my ears ring like an alarm bell. My eyes closed at the sound of the shot. When I opened them, Ameena was slumping to the floor, her hands clutching her stomach.

She landed on her back, blood pulsing through her fingers. Her breath came in rasping gasps and her eyes swam with tears, but she didn't scream. Not once.

'Oh, *now* look what you made me do,' my dad muttered. I dropped to my knees beside Ameena. The blood pumped out of her. So much blood. So much pain written across her face.

'It's OK,' I told her. 'You're OK. It's going to be OK.'

She shook her head. 'You're s-such a terrible liar,' she whispered, then she let out a groan. Her eyes swam, then focused. 'Tried to warn you. Told you n-not to come. Wanted us t-to run away. Together.'

'We can,' I said. I lifted her hand and pressed it to my face. Her blood was warm against my skin. 'We will. You're going to be OK. All that other stuff, it doesn't matter. It wasn't your fault. None of it was your fault.'

'Oh, God, this is sickening,' my dad mumbled. 'Excuse me while I puke.'

'Shut up!' I spat, hot tears stinging my eyes. 'Shut up!'

'Too late,' Ameena croaked. 'Too late. S-sorry. N-never wanted to hurt you. Wasn't as s-strong as you. Couldn't... couldn't fight him.'

Her face was becoming an ashen shade of grey. The carpet was awash with her blood now. It seeped out around us in a steadily widening circle.

'Hold on,' I pleaded. I pressed my hand against her stomach to try to stop the blood flow, but felt her life ebb out through my fingers. Her eyes rolled back in her head. 'Ameena!' I shouted, shaking her. 'Hold on!'

'Oh, what's the point?' my dad sneered. 'If you're going to die, just get on with it. Some of us have things to do.'

'D-do you t-trust me?'

'Yes,' I said. Despite everything that had happened in the last few hours, despite every suspicion I'd harboured from the start, I said, 'Yes.'

She smiled, then a jolt of pain made her go rigid in

my arms. She was shaking like a hypothermia victim, her body going into shock and shutting down.

'This s-stings a bit,' she said, when the convulsions had passed.

'I know, I know. But you'll be OK,' I said. I was fooling no one. We both knew what was going to happen. We both knew that this, finally, was the end.

'Have to tell you s-something,' she whimpered. 'Been t-trying to make you realise since the hospital. Y-you're too damn stubborn.' She gestured with her head for me to lean in closer. I felt her breath against my cheek as she whispered in my ear. 'This isn't the Darkest Corners. J-just looks like it.'

It took a moment for her meaning to sink in. I leaned back and stared at her, my eyes two circles of surprise. 'But that means...'

She nodded and her face lit up with that crinkle-nosed grin.

'Means what?' my dad asked. 'What did she say? Isn't she dead yet?'

'You d-don't have to be a-afraid any more,' Ameena whispered, squeezing each word out with the last of her strength. 'There's n-nothing left to lose.'

'What are you saying? What are you telling him?'

'Go get him, k-kiddo,' Ameena wheezed, and then the hand on my cheek became limp. Became lifeless. Her head tilted, just a tiny fraction, to the right. Her eyes didn't move, but they stopped looking at me, or looking at anything, for that matter.

And like that, the best friend I had ever had left me.

'Finally,' my dad sighed. 'I didn't think she was ever going to go. Now, where were we?'

Ameena's final few words chimed in my head. This wasn't the Darkest Corners, it just looked like it. I'd brought the barrier down, but the world hadn't changed. It had simply been filled with monsters. This was the real world. My world. And it had been all along.

And there it was, like a candle in the darkness. A single spark lit up inside my head.

My stomach twisted. I felt sick. Not because I was

powerless to stop what was happening, but because I *could* have stopped it any time I wanted.

Slowly, I stood up. I turned round and saw my dad smirk. 'Ah, yes, this is where we were,' he said.

His finger tightened on the trigger of the gun.

A hundred billion bright blue sparks roared inside my head.

Chapter Nineteen

THE END OF THE BEGINNING

I saw the bullet. First the metal, then the structure of the metal itself – not smooth, but pitted and ridged like some grey alien landscape.

Then deeper. I saw chains of molecules all latched together like an intricate web.

Deeper. The very atoms that made up the bullet, spinning like galaxies in a little lead universe.

I saw the bullet's kinetic energy, felt its heat, saw and understood the chemical make-up for the gunpowder that trailed in its wake.

And it didn't stop there. I saw the gun, all its individual components, and I knew how they worked.

I saw Ameena's blood on the carpet, heard Billy's whooshing through his veins.

Above that I heard simultaneously the chittering of microscopic dust mites and the screams of a whole world filled with the dead and the dying. I looked through the eyes of every living creature on Earth, saw what they saw, felt their fear and their panic and their utter hopeless despair.

By the time I'd done all that, the bullet had almost finished travelling along the barrel of the gun. I stopped it existing, then I did the same to the gun itself. Neither one disappeared in a puff of smoke. There was no theatrical flash. Both bullet and pistol simply ceased to be.

My dad looked at his empty hand. Thirty-three muscles in his face conspired to make him frown. Then he looked back at me, his pupils dilating as fear flooded his body with adrenaline.

'Ah, so that's what she told you.'

'You killed her,' I said. I watched the sound waves ripple lazily away from my mouth. They wriggled like tiny snakes through the air. 'You killed Ameena.'

'For your own good,' he said. 'I did it for you, son. Don't you see? I've done everything for you. To help you unlock your full potential.'

'Stop talking,' I said, and he did. He had no choice in the matter. 'The power. You said it was god-like.' I flexed my hands and felt whole ecosystems thriving between the cracks of my skin. 'You have no idea.'

I allowed him to speak again. 'Exactly, son! There's nothing we can't do together. Nothing we can't accomplish.'

'I could take you apart,' I told him. 'One atom at a time, I could take you apart and spread you across the world. I could do that, you know? Just by thinking it.'

He shook his head and laughed. 'Yeah, but you wouldn't. You're a *good boy*, Kyle,' he said, using the words as an insult. 'Your mother brought you up soft. Even after everything I've done, you haven't got the guts to kill me. Oh, sure, you say you're going to. You come looking for me, but you don't have the stomach for it. You're weak. You're *pathetic*.'

'I'll do it,' I said.

'Go on then,' he barked, fury suddenly etching the lines of his face. 'Do it. Kill me. I murdered your mum, turned your grandmother into a monster, shot your girlfriend right there in front of you! So come on, tough guy. Kill me. Do it.'

I clenched my fists. I wanted to kill him. More than anything, I wanted to.

But I couldn't. I couldn't just slay him in cold blood. That would make me no better than he was. The screechers in the church, the monster I'd battered with that rock – I had no choice. That was survival. This would be different. This would be murder.

He chuckled at the back of his throat and stepped past me. I flinched as he patted me on the shoulder. 'Didn't think so,' he said, then he trotted down the stairs, hands in his pockets, as if he didn't have a care in the world.

'I can't kill you, but I can stop you,' I told him, following. He did a twirl at the bottom and made for the door.

'You could, but what would be the point? You don't

have the guts to finish me off.' He stopped and met my eye. 'Do you really want me around? Whispering into your ear, telling you about every terrible thing I've done?'

I had no answer for that. His smile widened. 'Thought not.'

He skipped on the spot, then carried on towards the door. 'It's not over, you know. I'll think of other ways to make you suffer. You may be all-powerful, but you've still got a heart beating in there, and I can still break it. And you'll still be too much of a goody two-shoes to stop me.'

The door opened and I.C. came staggering in, breathing heavily. He crashed right into my dad, who hissed with annoyance.

'Whoops. Sorry, mister,' I.C. said.

My dad grimaced. 'You will be, you little runt,' he said, and he swung a clenched fist at I.C.'s cheek.

A hand clamped round his wrist, stopping his arm dead. My dad looked up into the narrowed eyes of Mr Mumbles. Mumbles forced him back into the room and kicked the door closed behind him. Outside, the howls of the monsters rose in volume.

'Let go of me, *freak*,' my dad spat. Mumbles twisted his grip and my dad yelped in pain. His hand bent in towards him, forcing him to his knees.

'Name-calling is bad. Isn't that right, I.C.?'

'That's right, Uncle Mumbles.'

My dad snorted. 'Uncle Mumbles? You've got to be kidding me.'

Mumbles raised his eyes to me. I stood on the stairs watching. For all my power, I felt completely helpless.

'Thought the plan was to kill him?'

I lowered my gaze. 'I... I couldn't.'

'He's too weak!' my dad snarled. 'Too pathetic. He couldn't do it. Can you believe it? After everything I did, he couldn't finish me off!'

Mumbles looked at me for a long time, then his eyes went down to the man kneeling before him. 'He's a good kid. Even after what you've done, he's a good kid.' He leaned down so his face was next to my dad's. 'Me? Not so much.'

With a roar, my dad's free arm lashed out. I saw the blade in his hand, but he moved too quickly, taking me by surprise. It sliced upwards, stabbing straight for Mr Mumbles' stomach.

'Look out!' I yelped.

There was a blur of movement. I saw Mumbles' hands on my dad's head, and then they jerked sharply. I heard bone splintering and the knife thudding on to the carpet. Mumbles stepped back and my dad's broken body slumped face-first on to the floor.

'Sorry you had to see that,' Mumbles said.

I stared at him, then at the man on the carpet, his head twisted at an impossible angle. My father, maybe, but not my dad. Never my dad. I shrugged and drew in a shaky breath. 'I'm not.'

I returned to the upstairs landing and looked down to where Ameena lay. I couldn't bring her back. I knew that. I could restore her to life, yes. Reanimate her so she walked and talked like Ameena, but it wouldn't be her. Not really. Just like it wasn't my mum earlier. The dead stayed dead, and there was nothing I could do about it.

But there were other things I *could* do.

Billy was still unconscious, but he'd be awake in a few minutes. That was more than enough time.

I walked down the stairs and stood between I.C. and Mr Mumbles. I made a point of not looking at the body on the floor.

'What now?' asked Mr Mumbles.

The front of the house folded up like a map, revealing the world beyond. A near-perfect circle of snow blanketed a patch of the street. Several dozen creatures stood frozen atop it, their bodies encased in frost and ice. But hundreds more raced for the house, leaping and bounding and slithering and scampering, all closing in for the kill.

'You broke your house,' I.C. said.

'Nice trick,' Mumbles added.

'I can feel them,' I said. 'Every one of them. I know what they are, who they were, where they came from.'

'What, all of them?' Mumbles asked, unable to hide

the surprise in his voice. 'There must be two hundred out there.'

'No, *all* of them,' I said. 'Everything that came from the Darkest Corners. I'm inside their heads.'

I.C. jabbed a finger in his ear and wiggled it about. 'Hello? Hello? Are you in there?'

The things out in the snow were moving at a fraction of their actual speed now. I held them in slow motion until I was ready to deal with them.

'I can send them back,' I said. 'All of them. I can send them back to the Darkest Corners and rebuild the wall.'

Mumbles nodded. 'Then do it.'

I hesitated. 'But there'll be nothing to stop it happening again. If I send them away, then use my abilities, I'll reopen the gateway and they'll all come straight back through.'

'Then don't use your abilities.'

'I... I'm not sure I can stop. I don't know how to switch them off. I've got the power to save the world, but my next thought could destroy it all over again.' I looked to Mumbles for help. 'What do I do?' I pleaded. 'What do I do?'

There was a lingering, drawn-out silence. I.C. was the one who finally broke it.

'You could come and live with me and Big Nose,' he suggested. 'He smells a bit funny, but he's nice.'

Mr Mumbles and I exchanged a long look. He ground his teeth together, as if chewing the idea over. 'You'd be powerless,' he said at last. 'Helpless. And they'd all be after you. They'd all want revenge.'

'But we'd look after you. Wouldn't we, Uncle Mumbles?'

My old imaginary friend regarded me impassively. And then, finally, he gave an almost imperceptible nod of his head. 'Yeah,' he said. 'Why not?'

I remembered the photograph I had found in Joseph's wallet, back when I was trapped in Doc's hospital in the Darkest Corners. It was a photograph of me, Mumbles and I.C. together. It had confused me at the time for all kinds of reasons, not least because I looked older in the picture than I was at that moment.

How many years would it be, I wondered, before that photograph was taken?

'Maybe... we can make it better,' I said. 'There are good people there, I can feel them. They're scared. They have to go back, but maybe we can help them. Maybe we can fix things.'

'The Sheriff of Monster World,' Mumbles said. He shrugged. 'I'm game if you are.'

I closed my eyes and time returned to normal speed, but the things outside didn't move. Blue strands of electrical light trailed from my fingertips. They spread out like an endless web, passing through the bodies of the creatures in the village, the town and beyond.

On and on they went, streaking through countryside, through cities, across countries and continents until a network of shimmering blue crisscrossed the whole world.

I would send them back, but there were some things I had to do first. Some things I had to fix. I focused.

Upstairs, a door opened. A little girl emerged to find her brother lying fast asleep on the floor.

'Billy? Billy, wake up.'

I heard the scraping of Billy's eyelids flicking open, the tightening of his throat, the racing of his heart.

'Lily? Lily, you're OK? You're OK!'

I smiled. I couldn't bring back the dead, but I could fix the living. I could undo the damage that had been done. Not just Lily; the others too. All the screechers, human again, back to the people they once were. The fires extinguished too, the burned-out buildings restored, all with just a thought.

I turned my attention to the fiends I held frozen.

'You are not supposed to be here,' I said, and my voice carried silently around the globe. 'It's time you all went home.'

I imagined a door thrown open wide enough for us all to pass through.

I imagined a door leading through into an eternity of darkness.

I imagined a door closing behind us, sealing us off from the world where I had once belonged.

The blue strands disappeared. Something inside me went *whoosh*, and I suddenly felt very small. I could no longer hear atoms rubbing together. Could no longer see through any eyes but my own.

Angry shapes moved in the gloom around me. A swirl of frosty mist prickled goosebumps on my skin.

'What now?' I whispered.

'Now?' said Mr Mumbles as his fingers tightened on my arm. 'We run.'

And run we did.

Together.

THIRTY-FOUR DAYS
EARLIER...

EPILOGUE

What had I expected to see? I wasn't sure. It had been a long time, after all.

How many decades was it since I'd stood on this spot? Five? Six? Time had little meaning in the Darkest Corners, and I'd stopped counting the days a lifetime ago.

I breathed in through my nose, tasting the air. Fresh air. Real air.

Real world.

I ran my hand across the reception counter and caught my reflection in its polished sheen. Most of my hair had gone years back, but the moustache had been blossoming nicely for the past few months. I looked exactly as I remembered.

Coming back was risky. I almost didn't, but *he'd* done it – *I'd* done it – already. Once I'd realised that, I knew I had no choice. Everything had already happened, after all. Coming back was my destiny. I'd seen it with my own two eyes.

The rain hammered down against the big windows of the police station. I remembered that rain. Even after all these years, I could still feel its icy sting on my skin.

There came a sound like thunder, but not thunder. It was the sound of a man in a hat being punched through a garage door. I remembered that too.

I had plenty of time, but then I always had plenty of time these days. I had control over it. I could ride it like a tramline, changing speed and direction whenever I liked.

I could've gone anywhere, any*when*, but certain things needed to happen in the right place at the right time, otherwise things might not work out the way they were supposed to. Joseph had told me that before he died. Before I realised who he was.

A spark fluttered and time skipped forward. In the distance, a stone donkey exploded. Not long now.

Uniform, I thought, and I was wearing it before the thought had fully formed. I looked down. Slightly ill-fitting, just as I remembered.

There was the hot chocolate, of course. Couldn't forget that. It appeared without a sound on the countertop, all marshmallows and sprinkles and thick whipped cream.

I could hear footsteps, two sets, racing along the windswept street. Just a few more seconds. I felt my pulse begin to quicken.

The Christmas cracker appeared in my hand just before the door flew open. I pictured the little rectangle of paper inside it, the single word printed in bold black print across it:

DUCK

The hat! I'd almost forgotten the hat. A little pointed shiny one, held under my chin by a string of thin elastic. It popped into existence just as a rain-sodden boy with panic in his eyes staggered into the station.

'Ho-ho-ho!' I said, and I saw the disappointment register on his face. 'Merry Christ—'

'Someone's trying to kill us!' he blurted.

'Oh,' I said, letting my shoulders sag. 'That's put a dampener on that then. Been waiting all day for someone to come in and pull that.'

The boy stared at me as if I were mad. He looked so young. *I* looked so young. I set the cracker down on the counter and fought the urge to tell him about his future. About *our* future.

He couldn't know. He couldn't know that I was him and he was me, just many years apart. He had to figure it out on his own. And he would. One day.

'Sorry,' I said, and I managed a smile for the boy I had once been. 'You were saying...?'

ACKNOWLEDGEMENTS

And that's it. Done. Finished. Over. Five years after I started writing it, Invisible Fiends is complete. The series would not have been possible without the help of lots of amazing people, and while I don't have the space (or the memory) to thank every one of them individually, I've singled out a few:

My agent, Kathryn Ross, who first saw promise in an early draft of *Mr Mumbles*.

Tommy Donbavand, the man who suggested I try writing children's books in the first place. Good call, Tom.

My editors at HarperCollins Children's Books — Nick Lake (books 1-3) and Harriet Wilson (books 4-6), who told me when to put motorbike helmets on children, and when to remove hooks from clowns' faces.

Everyone else who worked at HarperCollins over the course of the series, particularly Geraldine Stroud, Catherine Ward, Tiffany McCall, Rosi Crawley and Mary Byrne, who all did their best to ensure I didn't get lost and/or die while on tour. They mostly succeeded too.

I'd also like to thank the fantastic people at The Scottish Book Trust, the teachers and librarians who invited me into their schools, the bloggers who wrote about the series and the booksellers who sold it.

My family should get a mention too, for all their support and occasional withering criticism – particularly Fiona, who I proposed to on the dedication page of book one. In case you were wondering, she said 'Yes'.

Finally, and most importantly, I'd like to thank you, dear reader, for sticking with Kyle and Ameena through all their adventures. You really are lovely. No matter what anyone else says.

Printed by RR Donnelley at Glasgow, UK